Nugget
in a
Nutshell

GW00716675

by

Dennis Bailey

Throughout his life the author has
noted happenings which, to him, suggested
a deeper meaning. These stories and events
he has reduced to short talks, some of
which he has used in church, at School
Assemblies and on the radio

Illustrated by

Rod Hague

**Dedicated to my three delightful grandchildren:
Solomon, Samuel and Hannah**

Printed by Reproprint, Alderholt, Fordingbridge, Hampshire, SP6 3AA

Acknowledgements

I am very grateful for the help given by my family in writing this book, particularly my wife, Margaret, who has encouraged and given me every assistance.

To Rod Hague who so willing agreed to draw the sketches. Like the stories themselves they vary in style and mood but I believe add greatly to the interest and meaning of them.

Many thanks to Valerie Allpress and Patricia Alexander who have corrected grammatical errors and made helpful suggestions.

I would like to thank Eric Jennings whom I asked to read the manuscript and tell me of anything that jarred his sensitivities, particularly from a theological or humanitarian standpoint. There were a lot of marks with a red pen but most were appreciative and encouraging!

Thanks also to BBC Producer, Clair Jaquiss, whose encouragement prompted me to write scripts for her "Pause for Thought" programme. It was these that form the basis of this collection of stories. Clair has also written a Foreword to this book for which I am very thankful. My thanks also go to Mark Jackson and Cathy Bennett of Reproprint who have given much help and advice regarding the printing. I would also like to thank those people who have allowed me to use stories about them. In a few cases the names have been changed to disguise their identity.

None of the above named necessarily support or agree with all of the text in this book.

Contents

Inspired by Friends

Christmas

A Pondering "Preacher Man"

Easter Garden

Thoughts from New Zealand

Sermon Remembered

Thinking Aloud

Epilogue

Bibliography

The publications are listed below with the associated pages in this book

The Book of Mission, Past and Present, (1857) Edited by L.N.R and dedicated
to the British & Foreign Bible Society
The Glories of Salisbury Cathedral, (1953) Jeffrey Truby
Winchester Publications Ltd. Page 35
Congregational Churches of Dorset, (1899) W. Densham and J. Oggle.
W.Mate & Sons Ltd, Bournemouth, Page 35
Primitive Methodist Magazine February 1845, Page 69
It happened in Palestine, (1936), Leslie D. Weatherhead
Hodder and Stourton Page 78
Cruden's Complete Concordance to the New and Old Testament, (1930)
Lutterworth Press.   Alexander Cruden, Page 101
A Shepherd Remembers, (1937) Leslie D. Weatherhead Page 104
Woodbine Willie, a study of Geoffrey Studdert-Kennedy, (1962)
William Purcell, A.R. Mowbray, Oxford & London, Page 110
My Life with Martin Luther King Jr, (1969), Corretta King,
Hodder and Stoughton, Page 124
Daily Readings from W.E. Sangster, (1966)
Edited by Frank Cumbers.
Epworth Press Page 129
How to live to be 100, (1975) Dr J.A.S.Sage, W.H.Allen & Co. Ltd. Page 133
Circuit Life, Salisbury. Fred Jones, Page133
Commentary on Matthew, David Smith, Hodder & Stoughton, Page 78
New Zealand, Insight Guide, (1993) Edited by Gordon Mc Lauchan,
APA Publications (HK) Ltd. Page 111

The following Internet sites have also been helpful
Hungersite Web site Page 141
Department of Health www.info.doh.gov.uk/ Press release 2002/0419, Page 143

Rod Hague

Rod Hague was born in Hampshire in 1947. His artistic abilities were recognised from an early age and as a young boy remembers sketching members of the congregation in the village Methodist chapel. He attended Salisbury College of Art in the sixties where he studied Commercial Art and Design.

Drawing and painting have been his main occupation for most of his working life during which he has exhibited regularly in one man and mixed exhibitions in London and the provinces. He has also exhibited several times at the Royal Academy. His work has sold privately, in galleries and to publishers. He lives near Fordingbridge, Hampshire and has known Dennis Bailey for over fifty years and was very pleased to contribute to this book.

Preface

This is a book of happenings and observations which have literally set me thinking about deeper meanings. Some are humorous, others tragic but they make up the variety of experiences which we all meet in everyday life. Here I have tried to extract "nuggets" of truth which have glistened for me as I have set them "in a nutshell".

My father was a superb storyteller. During the 1939/45 war, on his weekends home from a Spitfire factory, he would relate to us things which had happened in his work or the story of a film he had seen and he would keep us children spellbound.

So, as a child, I came to appreciate the value of stories and, further, that they sometimes had a double meaning. At Sunday school and church I heard the Parables of Jesus which so powerfully conveyed a hidden meaning. Later, when I became a lay preacher, stories with a meaning fascinated me and I remembered them or saved the newspaper cuttings, which have been a resource for preaching ever since.

The late renowned Methodist preacher, Revd Derrick Greeves, a former minister at the Methodist Westminster Central Hall, was a king at using apt stories in his sermons. People would say, "Where does he find his perfect illustrations?" Derrick showed me himself. They didn't just float into his mind. Every morning when he found a story in the newspaper, when he was reading a book or when he had a personal experience, he would meticulously paste or write it into a yearbook under different headings. Derrick's inspiring sermons and broadcasts were the result of a lifelong discipline to record the parables of everyday life.

My collection of ideas and stories, I'm afraid, are not so well ordered, but since possessing a computer I have endeavoured to record them as they came to mind.

Encouraged by the acceptance of some scripts for the Radio 2 "Pause for thought" programme and the support given me by the producer, Clare Jaquis, I continued writing short, simple talks with a message. Some of these I have broadcast; others I have used in school assemblies and sermons. Wherever, the aim has always been to enlighten, enrich and hopefully to acquaint folk with the person and nature of Almighty God as revealed in Jesus.

This book contains a collection of these talks together with some items that I can only describe as personal "hobby horse" thoughts which I have been aching to express somewhere for years.

My prayer is that these thoughts will cause the reader in some instances to smile, but always to reflect and hopefully respond in some way - even if it is only to say, "Who on earth wrote this?" Perchance a story might resonate in someone's mind, inspiring him or her to think about life on a higher plane and seek to know more about this person, Jesus, whom I try, often so inadequately, to follow.

I also hope that the stories will be repeated as illustrations in talks, sermons and school assemblies, and for this reason I have included an index to help the speaker find one suitable to a particular theme.

The stories marked * were broadcast nationally on BBC Radio2 Night-time 'Pause for Thought' programme at 1.30am and 3.30am or Saturday 'Pause for Thought' at 6.30am.

I am now, regularly broadcasting the "Morning Thought" on BBC Radio Solent. This book was compiled before I started the new undertaken which is quite a challenge too, for now I have to compact my thought into ninety seconds! By rewriting many times and with clever editing by the producer, Dave Adcock, I have, hopefully, managed to convey something meaningful to local listeners.

June 2005

Foreword by
Clair Jaquiss
BBC Producer and Broadcaster

That little phrase "Pause for Thought" brings with it all kinds of wisdom: that moment just before the front door closes with your keys inside, or the point just before you fill in that blank application form or start that novel, or the silence before you give your answer to the person who has asked you to marry them.

The world of broadcasting isn't compatible with silence, but *Pause for Thought* is paradoxically about a kind of silence at least – words of silence in the middle of the usual hubbub of music and opinion, laughter and news. I don't mean I want to hear sanctimonious piety. That may make me pause for thought, but for the wrong reasons. I don't want to hear something that has no connection with my life or my feelings either. Those brief minutes are an opportunity for refreshment, stimulation or quirkiness that takes me out of my world for a moment, and returns me changed or even renewed.

Dennis's thoughts are like that. He follows in a fine tradition of storytelling that makes a point for the people who hear it, that respects their intelligence by allowing them to make up their minds and then try out living the implications of the story. He has the skill to open people's eyes to the significance of things that happen in their own world. Dennis's thoughts spring from his own deep spiritual relationship with God and life that finds meaning in all kinds of experience. That's what we developed together in our Pause for Thoughts for late night on BBC Radio 2. Sometimes they worked well. Sometimes we spent a lot of time rewriting or cutting scripts down to time and always for their own good. I valued his patient humility, gentleness and passionate integrity that comes through so powerfully in his talks. My one regret is that in reading these thoughts you will miss the soft tones of his voice painting the picture and drawing you into the characters and their stories.

Anyway – enough of this. A friend once said, "Don't ask me to *Pause for Thought*, I'd be much better off with something called "For goodness sake get on with it". Take that advice. Turn the page.

All in a day's work

A Chain Reaction

If I mention the word 'accumulator', the majority of people would think I was talking about a lottery or betting ticket. A few would immediately think of a square jar with two terminals on the top, filled up with sulphuric acid. Fifty years ago thousand of homes relied on these two volt cells to supply the low tension power for their radio, or wireless sets as we called them then. I worked in a radio repair workshop. Downstairs was a charging room where every day hundreds of these accumulators were being recharged under the supervision of a lad called Peter They were placed on slate covered shelves which were stacked from floor to ceiling around the room and were each linked to the other with wire. Perhaps they were in a chain of fifty to a hundred cells. One day we heard the most terrible prolonged crashing. It seemed as though it would never end. We rushed downstairs to find a most dreadful yet, at the same time, ironically amusing scene. There was Peter squat in the middle of the floor holding his head in his hands, surrounded by dozens of broken accumulators. There was glass and sulphuric acid everywhere. We literally doused him with water to dilute the acid. Fortunately, although his overalls did go into holes, he didn't suffer any burns. It was all because he had tripped over a wire and the domino effect had occurred, a chain reaction where one accumu-lator pulled down the next. One little mistake and the results were cruel. Not only was there the loss of customers' accumulators which they needed to operate their radio, but there was the monetary loss to the firm - and in those days Peter's job was on the line, too.

As I think about it now I am reminded of times when I have set off such a reaction just by opening my mouth and saying something which, if I had thought about it a bit more, I would have held my tongue. Just think of some of the politicians and media personalities who, recently, have made terrible gaffes. The effect has been, for them, catastrophic. In the New Testament John writes in his first letter: "The tongue, small as it is, can boast about great things. Just think how large a forest can be burnt down by a tiny flame and the tongue is like a fire". To put things right afterwards is almost impossible, for what we say can never be unsaid. Sometimes, perhaps when we are having a disagreement with someone, we get a bit worked up and say the most hurtful things to the people we love most. Many have regretted such ill chosen remarks for the rest of their lives. The best advice is to think before we speak.

I suppose that the same could be said of the pen, for what we write can also have unlimited repercussions for good or evil, so it does behove us to be guarded and think before we speak or write. Hopefully the next few pages of my thoughts expressed in writing will set off a chain reaction for good as the sentiments are remembered and repeated.

Removing the Mask

Some faces you see and forget directly; others remain in your mind forever. There is one such face which I can always recall, for it appeared on the front cover of a brochure advertising a product I sold some twenty years ago. I can describe the face now, so vivid was the impression made upon me, for it was a stunning picture of a beautiful girl.

Gorgeous round brownish eyes, flowing flaxen hair that swept round just above the eyes and cascaded onto the shoulders, framing a face which just hinted at a smile. I must have seen hundreds of such captivating pictures before, but why then does this particular one remain in my mind?

It was like this. I was serving in the shop one day when in walked a sophisticated, attractive young lady with her equally attractive friend. Both of them were well turned out in obviously expensive clothes and were professionally made up with deep ruby lipstick, dark mascara and their cheeks suggesting a rather unreal blush. The lady asked me for something and as I turned away I was suddenly jolted to look back by an exclamation. "Look!" she said, "That's me," pointing at the brochure on the counter, "It's the first time I've seen it. May I have one, please?" "Of course," I said, giving her a handful. As I looked, I could easily recognise her as the same person who stared up at me from the brochure. She giggled as she pointed out the other pictures inside and related excitedly the fun involved in having the photos taken. In fact she was transformed. Her mask had well and truly slipped. From being a cool, sophisticated model she had become a bouncy, bubbly person, vibrant and warm. 'Just like the girl next door,' as we say, and I liked the change and will cherish the memory.

We are all to some degree the same, reluctant to let people know what we are really like. Only those who live and work with us have any idea of what lies behind our facade.

When the Samaritan woman encountered Jesus at the well, all the fences and barricades were up. It would have been surprising if they hadn't been. After all, the Jews in those days had no dealings

3

with the Samaritans. That the Jew was a man made the scene extremely unusual, as Jewish men did not speak to strange Jewish women, let alone a despised Samaritan woman. Furthermore, Jesus was known as a Rabbi so a Samaritan woman would feel very uneasy in His presence. Yet the conversation which started with Jesus asking the surprised women for a drink of water ended with her being frank and free in her talking. Her mask had slipped, too.

When we encounter Jesus today, he still can have that affect upon us. It's not only that he sees us for what we are. It's that, perhaps for the first time, we truly see ourselves.

"You'll soon get used to it"

How soon we become familiar with new things. Incidents, which were quite intolerable, in a short while we passively accept. When I related my story of a recent robbery, the reaction of so many people, far from being shocked, was: "What do you expect? It's happening everywhere!"

Some years ago I received a phone call from a customer saying that the television, which had just been repaired by my engineer, was worse than it was before. "The screen is covered with fine white lines," she said. On my engineer's return I enquired as to what he had done to the receiver. "I replaced a capacitor, which stabilised the field, and as the picture was terribly blurred I re-set the focus" he said. I called in to see the TV only to be presented with a first class picture. "What's wrong with it?" I enquired. "Can't you see?" said the husband, now getting exasperated. "The picture is covered with all those lines," he said pointing to the lines which make up the TV system. "We never had those before your engineer called." I then realised what had happened. I took off the back and adjusted the focus control just enough so that the lines tended to fuse together producing a blurred picture. Immediately I did it I knew I was on the right track because the lady, enthused with delight, said, "That's right. You've done it! Don't you send that other engineer here again. He doesn't know what he's doing!" I tried to explain that what he had done was correct and that the defocused picture she had got used to was wrong. Leaving a very bad advert of our work, I drove away dejected knowing that they had opted for the worst because that was what they had come to accept.

The trouble is that we all are like that to some degree. We become so used to things, which would have formerly been unacceptable, that we even begin to rationalise our tolerance of them. I find that my attitude to some TV programmes is far more liberal than it was a few years ago. "It's a different age," I say to myself, "and far healthier out in the open than being suppressed. One mustn't be narrow minded." Yet I don't feel comfortable about it. Is it just coincidence that at a time when there is a permissive mass media

5

there is a rapid decline in moral standards? We have become used to what is now called sleaze in every stratum of society. Our soap operas, films and plays almost imperceptibly nibble away at their guidelines on decency and propriety whilst we slowly become accustomed to the falling standard.

I can't help thinking that what it wants is a "repair man" to come and refocus society. That's it, we need a Messiah. Well, there was a Messiah named Jesus. What it needs, I think, is for each one of us to call Him into our lives and then society would be renewed. *

Churches Together

As a television engineer I was often immersed in the back of a receiver endeavouring to diagnose an obscure fault. It can be a lonely experience because, as you accumulate knowledge from your measurements and observations, you get hunches about where the fault lies but you would be hard put to rationalise your thoughts to a colleague. Included in the data which has entered your brain are all the past experiences of similar faults, the details of which have long been forgotten but lie there in the subconscious. It was while I was working on an elusive fault one day that my brain got its wires crossed completely. As I was thinking about the delay line, which is a device for slowing down some signals so that they all arrive at the cathode ray tube together, I said to myself, that's like the Methodist Church with all its committees. By the time the various bodies have met, the 'pot's gone off the boil'. At that point I looked at the loudspeaker and smiled to myself. That must be the Salvation Army, the noisy lot!

"Where can I find the Anglicans?" I said to myself and there staring me in the face were the synch separator circuits. Their job is primarily to assure that each line and field begins at the proper time. "Must be the Church of England. They're big in things being done in a disciplined and orderly way."

I was amused as I thought perhaps that the muting circuits, included to prevent extraneous noises being produced, might be the Quakers. Perhaps the line output transformer with its very high voltage which can emit incense might be the Roman Catholics but I realised that I was pushing the analogy too far. In any case, it was all a silly distraction and this repair had to be done.

It was afterwards that the thought came to me that all these circuits must work together to reproduce a good image of the trans-mitted signal on to the screen. So perhaps there is a meaning to my silly ruminations. If all the churches worked together, the image of God we showed to the world, would, I believe, be far clearer than it is today.

God wishes the world to know Him and the universal church

is his only institution set up to achieve this. I believe that the world will only see a clear picture of what God is like when the churches come together, not in boring uniformity, but in a unity of understanding and love.

I was given a book and began to read. *"The message of Divine Love cannot go forth without uniting the hearts and affections of those who receive it in simplicity and godly sincerity. If it breaks down the sin-cemented walls of separation between man and a justly offended God it will remove every barrier between man and his brother man! Christian Union! How frequently do we hear these words; but how seldom do we behold their realisation in the intercourse of life! How rarely do we see professing Christians act as though they were influenced by the Divine Spirit under whose teaching the great apostle to the Gentiles exclaimed. 'Grace be with all them that love our Lord Jesus Christ in sincerity'"*.

"What date was this book written?" I asked myself. To my amazement the British and Foreign Bible Society published it in 1857 and it began with a whole chapter on Christian Union which exposed the tragedy of separation.

At first I was pleased to think that there had been some progress, for at least the churches are doing things together and recognise each other but then the date of the book sank home. One hundred and forty five years have passed and we are still essentially only talking about unity.

My prayer is that, through the Churches Together movement, we won't be talking about Union for the next 147 years but that, from the grass roots, Christians will bring a new restlessness into the councils of all churches so that they will seriously seek avenues of understanding and unity.

CHURCHES
TOGETHER
in ENGLAND

Open to Scrutiny

I was dealing with a lady traveller in my shop one afternoon. Just as she was about to go she looked at me strangely and then said with some hesitancy "Excuse me but....". She stopped, blushed and then started to laugh not knowing whether to go on or not. "What were you going to say?" I prompted. " I--I think that you are wearing two ties," she said, "No," I said incredulously, " it must be the way the knot is tied." As I felt round the front of my collar I coloured up. "You're right," I spluttered as I lifted up two distinctly different tie tails. The front knot was sitting neatly over the smaller back knot. I can only think that when I dressed in the morning I put my tie on properly, saw another and, thinking I had forgotten to put one on at all, hurriedly put the second one on without looking in the mirror. The representative left still unable to control her laughter and I hate to think how many times she must have told the story on her rounds.

I went into the workshop where my staff were having their afternoon break and standing before them I said, "Can you see anything wrong with me today?" My sister started off. "Your jacket's beginning to look shabby." Another said: "You need a hair cut." "Your spectacles are bent." "One sideburn is lower than the other." So the observations went on, getting more personal every minute and I began to think that I must look a real freak. The humiliation was too much. "No," I said, "none of those remarks is what I'm talking about but do you know anyone else who comes to work wearing two ties?"

At this point I lifted the top tie with a flourish to a burst of convulsive laughter. I shall never forget that humiliating experience. I had laid myself wide open to their scrutiny and saw myself, from a physical standpoint, as they saw me. It's even more dangerous to invite people to say what they think you are like deep down.

I can't help thinking of the time Jesus went on retreat to Caesarea Philippi with his disciples. Jesus approached them and said, "Hi guys! Who do folks reckon I am?" They replied that some thought he was John the Baptist and others thought he was one of the

9

Prophets. "But how about you, who do you reckon I am?" asked Jesus leaving himself wide open for any reply. Without hesitation Peter replied, "You are the Christ, the Son of the living God." This was the momentous declaration but Peter didn't understand the significance of what he was saying. The disciples later began to see a side of Jesus they had never seen before. It was that His mission was to bring about the salvation of the world through suffering, dying, and rising from the dead - a concept quite contrary to what they expected.

Today, world wide, an increasing number of people would say that this same Jesus has transformed their lives as they saw him in a new light. He has leapt out of the stained glass window, walked out of the stilted statue, risen from the children's picture book, and become a radiant and vital friend and saviour. All because, still living dangerously, He places himself under our scrutiny with the question, "Who do you say that I am?" *

Family Fabric

"Look, a Fly"

When our children were young we went on a wonderful camping holiday to Switzerland. The weather was brilliant and the campsites were fantastic. I had been told that if we did nothing else we should be sure to take the spectacular mountain railway up the Jungfrau.

It surpassed all our expectations and the journey up was exciting with breathtaking views. Eventually we arrived at an observation platform near the summit.

I lifted Nicola up into my arms and marvelled at the stupendous panorama surrounding us. There were snow clad mountain peaks stretching out as far as the eye could see. I was spellbound, captivated by the wonder and greatness of it all and in my heart I was praising the God who made it. It seemed to me as though I was not just viewing a physical spectacle but that my soul was close to something even greater, something which I can only describe as "out of this world." I felt close to God himself. Just then I was forced back to reality. My daughter was calling me. "Daddy, Daddy," she cried. Her voice had a sound of urgency about it. "Look, look," she said. Nicola was pointing to something lower than the peaks surrounding us. I wondered whatever she was so excited about. " Look," she said, "a fly." I looked to where she was pointing and sure enough there was a common house fly sitting on the handrail. I brushed it away in disgust. Having paid the earth to see this breathtaking scene, the only thing my daughter could become excited about was a common fly!

The fly returned to another spot on the rail to the delight of Nicola but this time her excitement set me thinking. What right had I to disparage the object of her fascination? To begin with, the fly was within her experience. It was something she could relate to, whereas the mountains might as well have been a picture in a book, for she had no concept of size or grandeur. Also, this fly was a living creature, wonderfully made. It flew with speed and precision. God had created it for a purpose. Flies are part of the food chain and essential

11

to aid decomposition. I recall a chief of a Masai tribe in Kenya telling me that if the flies disappeared from their settlement, they would move on. Flies are not only an important part of God's creation, they are also a miracle of complex engineering. They have delicate yet exceedingly strong transparent wings, extremely perceptive eyes and a tough, pliable, external skeleton with tubular sectioned legs which are incredibly strong.

Ever since this mountain top experience, I think of flies as an even greater wonder than the peaks which I felt had brought me close to God. Nicola had taught me a valuable truth - to look at life through childlike eyes of wonder and recognise the awe-inspiring beauty, precision and perfection in the common everyday marvels of God's creation and to be thankful.*

Leave a Mark

In my wife's family there is a treasured possession. Some years ago when repairs were being done to the roof of a local hotel they discovered a ridge tile. Scratched into its surface, in beautiful copperplate script, was the inscription "W. Read, Maker, June 10th 1793"; one of their better known ancestors. As the family was then still in the associated business of brick making they were very pleased when eventually it was given to them. They could use it as an advert. It was often brought out just to show how well made their products were. Weather had thrown its worst at it. Hail, frost, snow, torrential rain and blazing hot summers had not even started to erode its surface. The best thing of all was that on the top of the ridge the maker had decorated it by pressing his thumb into the soft clay before it was fired - just as cooks will sometimes decorate the edge of the pastry on a pie. Today you can see every thumb impression so vividly that police could even use it as evidence in a court. William Read had left his mark on history. Even though it was only a roof tile, it was as tangible as Wren's St Paul's, Constable's Haywain or Hadrian's Wall.

I suppose all of us would like to think that we would leave a physical mark on history - something worthwhile that in years to come people would be able to recognise as ours.

One man who has certainly left his mark on history was Revd. Wilbert Awdry who, as was said in his obituary, will go down as "Thomas the Tank Engine Man". This ordinary, unassuming Church of England parson had invented a story about railway steam engines to amuse his sick son. He gave each engine a unique character which was based on his own love of locomotives. Later he wrote the story down and others were added. They were eventually published and now the twenty six books have sold some fifty million copies in a dozen different languages. Just think of the millions of children who have listened spellbound to their parents reading one of those fascinating stories.

What a mark he has made on history! Always to be known as

"Thomas the Tank Engine man". But was that how he wished to be remembered? Wilburt Awdry knew that there were more important, though less tangible, marks to leave and he hoped that people would remember him for more than just an entertaining story.

When asked how he hoped to be remembered he replied, "I should like my epitaph to say 'He helped people to see God in the ordinary things of life and he made children laugh'." *

()

"God won't like that!"

James, a five year old, had arrived at his Grandmother's house but couldn't wait to visit the chapel next door to see the workmen on ladders and scaffolding as they decorated the building. Closely supervised, he entered and surveyed the scene. His face changed from excitement to disgust. The decorators had painted the woodwork with a rather vivid undercoat. "Pink, pink," exclaimed James incredulously. "God won't like that!"

To James the colour was so shocking that God couldn't possibly approve. That is the God whom James, in his few short years, had come to imagine. Perhaps the popular idea of God being drab and dreary had already rubbed off on him.

But James is not alone in having restrictive ideas about what God is like. All of us tend to have preconceived notions, which often trap God in a straitjacket from which we have great difficulty in releasing him.

Many years ago we were returning home from a holiday in France and we saw before us a beautiful modern church, its white tower rearing up like a modern, sleek sculpture. We camped nearby determined that next day we would visit the building. The following morning, in the rising sun and against a brilliant blue sky, the tower looked even more impressive. As we approached and I prepared to film this modern edifice built to the glory of God, I was annoyed and shocked for the beautiful church was engulfed in mad activity. All the hubbub and noise of a French market was taking place immediately around its base. Gaudy carpets were stretched haphazardly against the sacred walls whilst smoke plumed above a barbecue from which blackened sausages were being sold. I noted giant watermelons, mis-shapen tomatoes, and onions of exhibition proportions sprawled with other vegetables over endless lengths of orange boxes. A metal loudspeaker exuded blaring pop music, salesmen competed for attention using horn type amplifiers and on countless stalls there was the babble of bargaining French traders and their reluctant customers. The cacophony of sound was enough to jar the ears of anyone, let alone someone seeking the peace associated with a church. I was disgusted and thought how God must be distressed, too. After all, didn't Jesus turn over the tables of the businessmen in the temple? There was no point in filming it now.

It was then that I believe God spoke to me. I didn't hear a voice but into my mind there came this thought which was in the form of words. "Where else do you suggest my church should be but in the place where my people work, shop, talk and generally go about their business?" It was a revelation to me for my idea of God and the place of the church changed from that moment. God is not removed from everyday life, for his incarnation should have shown me that he is vitally involved in it and that is where His church should be, too. *

Pilgrimage

"Is there any particular place you would like to visit?" was the question my sister put over the phone to her granddaughter in Canada who was about to leave for a two-month holiday in England. The reply left her speechless. "Please Grandma, may I go to Liverpool to see the haunts of the Beatles?"

Whether it should be considered a compliment I don't know but shortly afterwards my sister asked my wife and me if we would be prepared to take 15 year old April and her friend to see the places of interest connected with the famous four.

We decided it might be fun taking a couple of teenagers on their chosen holiday. Who knows! It might rejuvenate us. We planned to take them on a five-day tour in our camper van so that they would see a bit more of the British countryside than just Beatle country.

I must say I became increasingly excited as I contemplated the trip. I suppose, because I remembered so clearly the emergence of the Beatles, that sheer nostalgia about a period when my family and I were young explained some of my excitement. I recall listening to them for the first time and not quite knowing whether I approved or not. Somehow they represented the rise of teenage power and I wasn't sure that teenagers knew what was good for them. However they soon endeared themselves to us when our five-year-old son seemed to know the words and tunes before us "She love you Yeah, Yeah, Yeah," a little voice was singing all round the house.

Now here we were at the Albert Docks, Liverpool, with our delightful charges entranced by the presentation of the Beatle Story. In the afternoon we took a special tour of the city - visiting places like Penny's Lane and Strawberry Fields, now famous because of their mention in Beatle lyrics. We also saw the birthplace and homes of some of the Beatles and learnt that life had not been easy for these four exceptional boys. Perhaps some of their determination and resolution was forged on the hard road of suffering. I went along enthusiastically with this, filming the council house in which one of them lived and listening intently to the many personal stories our guide told - that is until I overheard a conversation. One guy said to another, "This is a pilgrimage I always wanted to do." This a pilgrimage! I was shocked, jolted. Who were these people? They were four extraordinary lads, but human. They would agree they made mistakes like the rest of us and openly admitted that they needed supernatural help to get the best from life.

I recalled a real pilgrimage I made to the Holy Land. I went to see the place where Jesus of Nazareth lived and worked. Now, here was an exceptional person. Without fault he loved and cared for people as no other and died a cruel death, I believe, to save the world.

Standing there viewing a semi-detached house in Liverpool I knew there was no comparison. Veneration is due to God alone and, thinking about it later a line for a song or more likely a hymn came to my mind. "Lets praise <u>Him</u>, Yeah Yeah Yeah Yeah".

Guernica

It would probably be our daughter's last holiday with us as hopefully she would soon be qualified. Then her career would dictate her holiday periods. We therefore asked her where she would like to go. "I would like to go to Spain to visit the art galleries and exhibitions," she said. Well, my knowledge on art is very limited and I wasn't too sure whether I would enjoy this - but Nicola would be with us and that would make up for it. To my surprise, I did find it enjoyable mainly because Nicola talked about some of the famous paintings. Soon, even I began to recognise the difference between a an el Greco and a Titian!

It was almost the end of the holiday when we reached Madrid. "Today I have something different to show you," my daughter announced. "We are going to see Pablo Picasso's famous painting called Guernica." I had heard of it, but Picasso's works were of no interest to me. I just didn't understand them. They were to my mind grotesque, gaudy and meaningless so I didn't enthuse over the impending visit.

What I am about to relate I am not proud of, for I entered quite prejudiced, determined that this wasn't for me. We walked down a corridor in which were displayed the doodlings Picasso had made prior to starting this painting. I didn't laugh audibly but I sniggered to myself as I looked at these hideous renderings. A banana-like hand, a head at an impossible angle to the neck, a bull with an eye under its ear and so on. By the time I reached the end of the corridor I was beside myself with suppressed amusement.

When we turned the corner we emerged into a large hall. There before us was the painting, black on white, just as though it had been painted onto a wide cinema screen. I couldn't take it in all at once. There seemed to be wheels and saw teeth, machinery and a chimney, people with dismembered limbs and grotesque horses all jumbled up. But above all I noticed that now a reverent hush had descended. My daughter had walked closer. I followed and noticed that this painting had moved her. She had tears in her eyes. "What is it, love?" I whispered. "Can't you see, Dad? Can't you see the agony in this

19

picture?" If it meant so much to her there must be something wrong with me. Nicola reminded me of how in the civil war a Nazi air squadron bombed the town of Guernica on the 26th April 1937. It was market day and over two thousand civilians were killed in just 3 hours. Picasso expressed his anguish in this picture and it has kept the memory of the crime alive. Now, as I looked at the painting, it did speak to me. I could see the agony and suffering, not only of the people of Guernica but of Coventry, Dresden and Hiroshima and the Crucifixion.

It was a precious though chastening experience - the day a father's eyes were opened by his offspring.*

A Point to Aim at

After a spell of wet weather my garden was looking quite uncared for but in one afternoon it was transformed. The reason was I had mown the lawns. I have heard it said, "If you cut the grass you can forget the rest." Well, of course, that is not strictly true but I know that once the lawns are cut I am once more in control. I'm on top and the garden is not on top of me. Actually, I think mowing the lawn is quite good for one. Depending on the size of your lawn and if you use the walking variety of mower, you must go miles giving yourself much needed exercise. Also, I find it a noisy time for contemplation. What else is there to do? It can be monotonous just walking up and down but I find myself thinking of all sorts of things and have known myself to stop mowing and run indoors to jot something down that had come to my mind which I might otherwise forget.

The other day while mowing I was reminded of my wife's late Uncle Ted, a countryman through and through. All his life he had worked on the farm and was renowned for his handling of horses. He used to boast of the wild, frisky yearlings which he "broke in", transforming them to obedient, willing pullers of the plough.

He came to my mind because I was trying to make the swathes behind my mowing straight. I was disgusted that they wriggled and curved the length of the lawn. In Uncle Ted's obituary it said that he was "satisfied with the simple things of life like a well stacked rick, a contented herd of cows and a straight furrow." As this thought came to me I could see one of the very ploughs he used, for he gave it to us and it is now a feature in our garden.

Once, in conversation with him, I asked him how he managed to plough a straight furrow. "Tis like this you, thee's got to get the fust furrow straight. What I'd da do is to take up the pleace where I be gwon-a start and pick out a spot tother side of the field in the hedge - maybe a tree or a fence post and looking at that I strike out keeping me eye on the point I be aiming at. If thee's do that thee's ul get a straight furrow. For mercies' seak don ee look just in front of the plough-shear or thee ul get a line like a dog's hind lag." I remember saying to him, "There must be a sermon in that somewhere, Ted." Now, as I was mowing, I put into practice Uncle Ted's advice and it worked. There was one half of the lawn with its disgraceful bendy lines and the others straight and true.

As you must have guessed, by the time that I had finished the lawn the sermon was fixed in my mind. We must look up and aim high in life if we wish to win through and leave something behind which others will appreciate. I believe there is no better way than to heed the writer of the book of Hebrews to "keep our eyes fixed on Jesus on whom our faith depends from beginning to end." *

The Call of the far Horizons.

Recently I have been transferring some old cine films onto video and was delighted to see again the film of my daughter, Nicola, actually making her first steps. I can recall now how one Sunday afternoon we were in the garden and Nicola was encouraged to walk by her seven-year-old brother. She was standing firmly holding her mother's hand when her older brother, Alistair, standing a little more than an arm's length away said, "Come Nicola, come." I was aware that she had begun to move towards him and I started shooting with my new camera. Diffidently she put her foot forward, still reluctant to let go, but her brother's encouragement was sufficient. She released her grasp and made her first step, stopped, tottered, and recovered balance. Alistair moved away so she began to walk again. And so it went on until after about five steps she tumbled into a heap of billowing dress and frilly underwear. The excitement of her family as they cheered and clapped is quite obvious even though it was a silent film.

About the same time, we were seeing on our television screens the bouncing figures of the astronauts making their historic first steps on the moon. Low gravity meant that they had to learn the art of walking again and these first steps, watched by millions, marked an important and exciting point in the history of the human race.

Last year we were celebrating the 25th. anniversary of man's first landing on the moon and it struck me, as I was making the video transfer of Nicola walking, that the two events were not unrelated. In both cases the participants were setting out on an adventure, reaching out to a new experience, exploring another dimension in their lives. They were both responding to what has been called "the call of the far horizons". That distinctive human characteristic, the natural desire to reach out to the unknown. It was Mallory, who subsequently died trying to conquer Everest, and who, when asked by a reporter "Why climb the mountain?" replied with what must be now one of the most hackneyed of quotes: "Because it's there."

23

When Jesus entered history he made known to us a loving God who presents to us, on our horizon, even greater mountains to climb. There are the mountains of injustice and prejudice - the mountains of avoidable suffering and pain - the mountains of starvation and homelessness, of war and violence. He came into the world not only to encourage us but He also actually climbed and conquered the mountain of selfishness, sin and death himself upon the cross. In so doing He was making a way whereby all of us might have the love in our hearts to conquer hatred and ugliness as He did. The fact that some mountains are still on the horizon waiting to be conquered is a sad reflection on us. However, let us not despair. The desire within us for a better world is the call of the far horizons beckoning us to strive for it. Let us pray for God's strength to reach out to bring this about.*

Remembrance

On the sideboard in the living room of the country cottage where I was brought up was a photo. It was of a soldier in uniform, Uncle Will, and opposite was a photo of his wife Auntie Emily, a chubby-faced, happy person. There was always a mystique about Uncle Will because he was dead - "blown to pieces" at Ypres during the first world war, we were told, with no grave or memorial. Mum used to tell us that, though he had only been married a year, he volunteered in response to Lord Kitchener's appeal because he didn't want to be labeled a coward. As we grew older Mum would tell us how, one day at the age of thirteen, she was nearing her home when she heard a wailing noise from the back door. She wondered what it was and ran down the path to see it was her mother lying on the step crying bitterly. She had just received a message to say Will had been killed. Mum's description was so graphic and her lips would always tremble as she told it.

His widow, Auntie Emily, lived at Bath where she had a shop which she ran almost single-handedly. It was difficult for her to visit us, but to my brother, sister and myself as children during the Second World War she was the "tops". She hadn't married again and had no children of her own but every Christmas she would send us a large parcel of toys. Auntie Emily never forgot our birthdays either, so our enigmatic thoughts of Uncle Will were more than counteracted by the vital reality of his widow who, though we had never met her, was very much alive and understood and loved children like us.

It was some forty years later that I came across a photo of a cemetery and written on the back were the words "Will's Memorial". We decided that we would try to find it on our next visit to the continent. From one military cemetery in the area to another we were directed and eventually knew by the photo that we had found the right one. Sure enough there on the wall was his name with thousands of others.

We opened the little safe by the side, took out the appropriate book and found the entry recording his death and his next of kin.

Sitting on a step reading it I was suddenly overcome with emotion and wept openly. Why? What for? I didn't have any of the usual memories, like bear hugs and football in the park. I couldn't have known him so what could he mean to me?

But somehow, through association, I did know him. My mother's devotion to her brother had somehow rubbed off on me and I knew I liked him and that he would have liked me. He was also special because of sweet Auntie Emily who honoured the memory of her husband of those few short months by constantly remembering his family.

We replaced the volume and, hand in hand, we walked down through the rows of head stones - but now every stone meant something. Each of them was another Uncle Will, a loved one who would be grieved over by a generation born years after the senseless carnage which shortened their lives.*

Living in Cloud-cuckoo-land.

Cloud-cuckoo-land, the place where only fools or children can expect anything to happen. The origins of this expression go back to a play written by Aristophanese (c.450-c.385BC) in which he refers to an imaginary city in the air built by birds to separate the gods from humans. The Greeks called it Nephelokokkygia i.e. Cloud Cuckoo Land. Certainly now it is used in all walks of life and is a favourite expression of politicians.

When Alistair, my son, was about eleven years old he was given a fishing rod and couldn't wait to use it. I remember vividly the day when he was preparing to go to a nearby stream in which you could often see a few trout. "Have you got a bag, dad?" he said. "What for?" I answered. "Don't be silly, to put the fish in of course" His face was beaming in anticipation of the expected catch as he rode off with his friend. I could have said that he was living in cloud-cuckoo-land for the likelihood of them catching any fish was very remote but, no, I was hoping they wouldn't be disappointed and perhaps I shared their excitement. Needless to say they came home with the bag empty but quite happy. They had seen "a big one" and might have caught it if they had used the right bait!

Unfortunately, many people have become so pessimistic and negative in their thinking that they can't believe that anything extraordinary might happen. I think this is sad as it not only makes their lives look grey and uninteresting but also disperses an aura of hopelessness. I say 'they' as if I am an exception but then I remember praying, month in, month out, for the end of apartheid in South Africa, for the dismantling of the Iron Curtain, for peace in Northern Ireland and that Tom should be reconciled to his brother Fred. If anyone were to suggest to me that by 1996 there would have been a peaceful transition to black rule in South Africa, that the Berlin Wall would have been torn down and that the Eastern Block of nations would have independence and free elections, that in Northern Ireland there would be a cease-fire and pending negotiations, and Tom and would make it up I might have replied, "Are you living in cloud-cuckoo-land?"

The almost magical attraction of children is their natural quality of excitement and expectancy typified by Alistair's fishing expedition. Perhaps that is why they were always so special to Jesus. They can't hide their excitement and anticipation of something wonderful happening. The grown ups in the crowd of listeners could be just as cynical and pessimistic then as now. Maybe there were some that were saying the equivalent of 'He's living in Cloud Cuckoo Land'. We might feel like saying that too, yet, deep down, we crave the excitement, simple trust, and confidence of a child.*

"I touched the Cross"

When we have visitors we often take them to our nearest building of exquisite architectural beauty, Salisbury Cathedral, which boasts Britain's tallest spire.   As we approach, my family begin to look at each other and mutter under their breath, "Wait for it, Dad's going to say it any moment now", and mouth behind my back what they are convinced I am about to say. Sure enough almost directly I oblige. "You see that cross up there on the top of the spire. I once touched the bottom of that." Our friends are suitably impressed and my family wink at each other. Of course, I know what's going on and secretly enjoy being the subject of their good-humoured fun. But let it be said that not many have touched the cross of Salisbury Cathedral spire and I am rather proud of my achievement.

When I think about it, I wonder how those few people who actually touched the cross on which Jesus had been Crucified felt about it afterwards. I wonder if Simon the Cyrenian ever looked back with satisfaction to the day he handled the crosspiece on which the sins of the world would be purged. There were the soldiers who lifted the cross up and Joseph of Arimathea who lowered it and took the body of Jesus and laid it in his own tomb. Did they remember the feel and texture of this infamous yet celebrated piece of wood?

Certainly it has been the practice of many pilgrims since to touch the replica crosses in cathedrals and shrines in the earnest hope that they might be cured of some ailment. However, in a very real sense, countless Christians since Christ died have felt that they have "touched the cross" and their contact was as real to them as if they had physically touched it. They have seen that their salvation from all that is bad was utterly dependent on what Jesus achieved for them on the cross in a great sacrifice prompted by love. So the cross and its message became so precious that they felt that it had touched them and had become the driving force in their lives.

It was at Athens, a highly civilised, artistic and cultural centre that St Paul preached to a cosmopolitan crowd. Because he knew that they were intelligent people, philosophers and thinkers, he appealed to them by means of an intellectual sermon. Some think that he wasn't wholly satisfied with this approach and therefore on arriving at Corinth resolved to preach "only Christ and his death on the cross". Whether this is the correct interpretation of Paul's attitude to his sermon in Athens is open to question but it cannot be disputed that from then onwards the message of the cross was the crux of his preaching and the central theme of Christian belief for without the cross the resurrection would lose its meaning.

No wonder an inspired and imaginative hymn writer wrote "so I cling to the cross, the old rugged cross".

We are leaving the cathedral now and one of our visitors inevitably asks, "When did you climb the spire?" With a whimsical smile I reply, "But I didn't say I climbed the spire. The cross was on view in the library prior to being hoisted to the top. I bent over the rope and touched it then!" My children nudge each other: "Dad must have his bit of fun!"*

Kindness

Occasionally, we all experience an outstanding act of unsolicited kindness which leaves us absolutely speechless. It must be some twenty five years ago, when our children were young, that a complete stranger did us a good turn for which we were so grateful, yet he left so quickly we hardly had time to thank him.

We had decided to drive up through the heart of London to visit the Tower but didn't realise that the Motor Show was on and that the traffic would be exceptional. All went well to begin with, and then we became utterly lost. A new flyover had been built and we found ourselves on an inside lane at a multi-lane junction waiting for the traffic lights to change but not knowing where to go. My wife had the map on her lap and must have looked concerned because suddenly we heard a voice bellowing from somewhere, "Where you going, luv?" It was the lorry driver looking down from his cab on her side. "We want to get to the Tower of London," she said. "Follow me," he replied. With that the lights changed and we moved off and at an appropriate moment I switched lanes and followed him. He took us off the main road on to smaller back roads. Twice he went through traffic lights which changed before we were able to follow him. Each

time when we eventually crossed, there was his lorry waiting for us. As we approached, his indicator signalled that he would pull out in front and continue to lead us. Finally he stopped, jumped out of the cab and ran back. "I've got to turn off now, but if you go straight on you will see the Tower of London and the parking signs. Hope you enjoy your visit." With that he was gone. A waving hand from his cab as he turned at the next junction was the last we ever saw of this true knight of the road.

Why should he have bothered? There was nothing in it for him other than a contented feeling that he had helped somebody. To us it was an act of sublime kindness which still moves me when I think of it. More so perhaps now, when the prevailing culture seems to be 'it doesn't matter who you hurt or tread on as long as you achieve your own aims'. It is as though, to be kind, is a sign of weakness when actually it is a symbol of strength because it often requires effort. When you experience kindness you discover it's secret - it is self-propagating and those who experience it are moved to show it themselves.*

Pulling Together

Dig for Victory was the slogan used during the war to encourage people to produce their own food. My father, who was away building Spitfires and only came home some weekends, became disturbed over the unused small field in front of our house. He decided that, as he hadn't time to dig any of it, he should ask a local farmer, Ed Lockyer, to plough it so that he could plant some potatoes. Now, this field hadn't been cultivated or even mowed for some years so the top turf was thick over a very light, loam soil. After inspection Ed said, "'Tis too tough on top vor one oss you, I zhal ave to git Marko to let I 'ave is 'oss to 'elp mine do it."

I was about eight at the time and remember Ed Lockyer and Mark Bailey from the adjacent small holding arrive with the plough and two horses. It happened to be the weekend my dad was home so we went out together to watch the proceedings. What ensued was nothing short of a pantomime for these two horses had never been hitched up together before. Because Ed had been asked to do the job, he was the one who started. "Gitty up there," he said bracing himself for the first movement. His horse started to move but the other stayed still. "Gitty up there," he shouted. Still one horse wouldn't move. Whether it was because Mark decided to give some instructions and his horse recognised his voice I don't remember, but suddenly he shot forward and the one which had been straining to go almost stumbled with the jolt, recovered and then they both lurched uncontrollably ahead at a phenomenal speed. Uncontrollable because Ed, who was quite short in stature, by this time was being dragged along on his knees. "Whoa, Whoa," he shouted trying to get to his feet and tugging at the reins. His horse heard the command and stopped dead The other horse kept going. The result was that the plough turned round in an arc and would have gone in a complete circle if Mark hadn't rushed up and grabbed the harness of his horse and stopped him. "Thy oss can't plough, ee ant got no sense." "Yes 'ee 'as," replies Mark, "Tis thine. Yer gie I the reins, I'll show thee." There then proceeded a near repeat performance, but Mark was fatter and was dragged around more on his stomach than his knees. By this time my dad was laughing so much he had tears streaming down his face and had to go in for fear of upsetting these honest countrymen who took pride normally in ploughing a straight furrow. They did complete the job with Mark leading his horse from the front and Ed behind the plough.

I suppose that is where the phrase "Pulling Together" comes from. In fact it is a very old idea because in the Bible we read about how unwise it can be to be unequally yoked. St. Paul warns the early Christians of the danger in marrying someone with conflicting beliefs. We all have heard how tortuous a home can be when husband and wife are pulling in different directions.

We have all done our share of matchmaking and marrying off couples whom we thought would make good partners and sometimes when the union has actually taken place we find we have been sadly mistaken. It would seem that sometimes the most unlikely couples turn out to make the happiest of marriages. What are the components which make these seemingly hopeless marriages work? I think one is an overriding sympathy and tolerance to the other person's point of view, without in any way compromising one's fundamental beliefs. This sympathy extends to not undermining another's position in front of the children and always looking for the best overall result in any argument. In fact, pulling together.

I didn't give the other component essential to happiness. It may seem sloppy and sentimental to mention it in this age of sophistication, but it helps a lot if a couple love each other. *

"I knew you'd come"

My mother's brother, Uncle Fred, had died and family and friends had gathered from a wide area to attend the funeral of this well-loved man. There was one exception, Auntie Rose, his sister; she lived 20 miles further on from the direction we came from. Well into her eighties, she felt too weary to get ready and make the trip down from the little terraced house where she lived on her own, although we did offer to collect her. The funeral was over and we were all about to return to our respective homes when I thought of Auntie Rose, a kindly little old lady, on her own thinking about all of us. I mentioned it to my wife and mother and immediately wished I hadn't because they were keen to visit her. It would double our return journey and, on second thoughts, I wasn't so keen on the idea but the face of this lovely lady, sad and lonely, haunted me so we decided to go. We tapped the door gently not to frighten her but she was there immediately, embracing us and ushering us in. We thought she would be surprised to see us, but no, she said referring to me: "I knew our Den would come." Little did she know how "our Den" nearly didn't come. I began to realise the frightening responsibility of living up to what people expect of us.

Perhaps we might never know the people we have disappointed, which makes me feel even more conscious of how sensitive to others I should be. Having said that, I think the responsibility is too much for me. I can't always be saying to myself: "What are they expecting of me?" Life would become unbearable. Perhaps their expectations are unreasonable and sometimes there might be conflicting pressures. It could be that sometimes people expect the worst from me though I suppose this could be a spur to me to prove them wrong.

Jesus reminded the impetuous disciple Peter that despite his promise to follow faithfully, he would deny his Lord three times. "Never in the world," exclaimed Peter. There never was a man who wanted to please his master and friend more than Peter the disciple. He was the one who rushed to defend Jesus in the Garden of Gethsemane, injuring a soldier with his sword and was reproved for his efforts. It was he who stealthily followed Jesus into the Judgement Hall – such was his desire to be close to his master in his time of trial. Then, when challenged by individuals who recognised him, he panicked and denied all knowledge of Jesus three times. The cock crew three times as Jesus predicted it would and Peter was heartbroken. He had let Jesus down; yet wasn't that what Jesus expected of him? The story goes on to say that Jesus turned and looked at Peter, who wept bitterly. It was as though Jesus was hoping against hope that Peter would stand by him and was sad for Peter because He knew he had such good intentions.

When I read of Peter becoming the great apostle who fearlessly proclaimed his faith, I am encouraged that one who initially, as Jesus expected, denied Him nevertheless fulfilled the outstanding expectancy of Christ and became the Rock on which God would build his church.*

Holy Places

The fortress was already overcrowded and filth encouraged fever which, in turn, was not helped by an inadequate water supply. The summers were gloomy as the height of the walls cast a shadow over the hovels within, and in wintertime the penetrating wind swept over the plain, its icy fingers delving deep into every corner. Yet in 1025 Bishop Herman was ordered by the king to move his see to this small miserable fortress called Sarum. He immediately began to plan a cathedral to be built within the fortress and eventually, after many setbacks, it was finished. Yet today it is in ruins, unheard of by many, because Bishop Richard le Porre in 1220 began the building of a new cathedral in the marshy land south of Sarum which would be more worthy of the God he worshipped. Salisbury Cathedral, so perfect an example of early English Architecture, was being born. Masons with mallet and chisel became master artists as imagination and vision gripped them. Viewed from any angle it has beauty and, as one who contemplates it regularly, I often pause in amazement as I see it in some new light - spot lit by the sun during a thunder storm or pointing its perfect spire heavenward through a shallow mist. It has been said of Richard le Porre that he planned to build a Church to the Glory of God but because he planned with genius the church became a Glory in stone.

Not fifteen miles from Salisbury in the county of Dorset, in a little hamlet with the quaint name of Cripplestyle, there stands a building also built to the glory of God that might well be called a Glory in mud. No, not architecturally but in what it represents, the fervour and devotion of a handful of godly, but uneducated country folk. I was born and grew up at Cripplestyle and I do not find it at all difficult to imagine what it was like at the turn of the 19th. century. These humble folk had a feeling of independence.

They owned their plot of land on a "lease for life" agreement from the Lord of the Manor and the "life" could be renewed on the payment of a small fine. Their lives were hard and habits primitive but they were independent. That plot of land reclaimed from the gorse and heather was virtually theirs, and they could do as they liked with it.

After a visit by some itinerant preachers of a Congregational body, a few friends gathered for prayer and learning in one of the mud cottages, down Pye Lane in fact. The nearest place of worship was some miles away. Religious interest grew until the hamlet was dotted with little cottage prayer fellowships which went some way to satisfy their need for spiritual nourishment. Their devotion was intense and it was inevitable that a time would come when some one would say, "We must have a church of our own so that we can meet and worship together". "But how can we afford to have a church built? Why not build it ourselves?" "That's it, friends - we'll build it ourselves". One of the brethren (my direct forefather - a William Bailey) offered a corner of his leasehold as the site and in 1806 work was begun.

It is recorded that the women, wives, sweethearts and children cut the heather and gathered it by day, and the men dug, transported and puddled the clay after a hard day's labour. While the women held the rushlights, the men built the walls laying the heather to bind the clay firmly together. The rafters and benches hewn out of oak were as rugged as the woodmen who swung the axes but the pulpit, angular and dignified, symbolised their reverence for the word of God. With the thatch neatly held with hazel spars and the interior whitewashed, how happy they were. Their labour of love was completed. They were to call it Ebenezer meaning "Hitherto has the Lord helped us". Ebenezer Chapel was the focal point of this scattered community. They organised a day school and pastoral oversight of the poor, ill and needy was part and parcel of their Christian concern.

How dare one compare Salisbury Cathedral with its splendour, symmetry and sheer size with Cripplestyle Mud Chapel with its higgledy piggledy windows - the former 750 years old, the latter a mere 160 odd years. Yet both were built to the Glory of God to communicate his love for man as shown in Jesus. The mighty and beautiful things in life will always impress. Salisbury Cathedral will always do something special for me. Yet as I sit on a nearby hill and contemplate the mud chapel nestled amongst a cluster of houses below I am impressed by something else: the simple, child like faith of those who built it and the fact that it undoubtedly fulfilled their need.

I wrote this talk in 1967 for Local Radio. (Though it was recorded it was never broadcast due to a sudden change in producers.) In 1888 a new large brick chapel was built up the road and

Ebenezer Chapel was only used once or twice a year. Sadly, after great efforts to preserve it, a corner of the roof caved in during October 1976. A long hot summer followed by a very wet autumn took its toll. The men from the Estate came to make the building safe and remove the thatch and burn it. Somehow the fire got out of hand and swept through the building. Lord Salisbury, to whom the land belonged, wished for a memorial to be built on the site and my brother and I with the help of the local people made a garden of rest

with a small plaque to explain the significance of the place. Over the years, the memorial deteriorated. In 1998 it was decided by the Cripplestyle Congregational Church to replace it with something more substantial and in May 2002 a fitting memorial consisting of a large Purbeck stone on which there is an inscription and a sketch of the chapel surrounded by a low brick wall was dedicated. I was privileged to give the address at this dedication.

The Chapel down the Hill. (See page 71)

A Personal Perspective

The Light went Out

Whereas visiting the Holy Land has been a disappointment to some, I didn't find it so. To me it was from start to finish a revelation, enhancing my imagination so often. The Bible was opened up for me in a remarkable way. Take for instance our visit to the Hezekiah's Tunnel in Jerusalem.

This feat of engineering was made by King Hezekiah in the 8th century BC. It's purpose was to bring water from the Gihon Spring to a point within the city walls during the Sennacherib invasion as related in the second book of Kings. A famous inscription found on its walls relates that the tunnel was started simultaneously from each end, the working parties meeting in the middle.

It is possible for the public to walk quite a distance in this tunnel coming out at the Pool of Siloam. A friend and I wanted to do this but we needed a torch. At the entrance there were boys offering to rent us a torch for an exorbitant amount but we decided to use my wife's small handbag torch. As you enter, the water is only ankle deep so we rolled up our trousers and started walking. The average width is 27inches (about 69 cm.) and the height varies as the tunnelling engineers used existing crevices and fissures wherever possible, hence the tunnel doesn't go in a straight line. Sometimes although the fissure went on straight the tunnel side-stepped left or right to connect with another fissure. We were about half way through with water up to our knees when disaster struck. The light went out. I don't suppose we were in real danger as another group was bound to come through shortly, nevertheless the darkness was complete. I have never before or since experienced such darkness. You could almost feel it. To me it was thick, oppressive and isolating. It was sealing us off.

I fiddled with the torch, took off the lens and tightened the bulb. Suddenly the tunnel was lit by what seemed a searchlight as the bulb made contact. Our exhilaration was spontaneous as we burst into shouts of hooray mingled with laughter. That little light was like salvation to us. It had penetrated our darkness. Now we could complete our walk. The water was to reach our thighs as we emerged into the Pool of Siloam. It was here that Jesus instructed the blind man to go and wash after he had made mud and smoothed it on his eyes. The man did as he was told, washed in the Pool of Siloam and returned seeing for the first time in his life, no longer to walk in darkness but granted the gift of light. Somehow that story means a lot more to me now.*

A Wider View

Bob was a countryman through and through. Although a brickyard worker, he spent all his life doing country things like fattening pigs, rearing hens and laying drains. Obviously he was intelligent but there was no higher education for him and he left school at 13 to work in the yard. Nevertheless, reading and his attendance at the village chapel increased his knowledge. Bob learned a lot from the preachers and passed all the scripture exams. His faith meant a lot to him and sustained him throughout his long but not uneventful life. His father had been a preacher of some local renown and Bob had always been in his shadow. People referred to him as 'old Sam Read's son'.

When I first came to know Bob I found him amusing. His prolific stories were usually witty and always entertaining. Often he would philosophise and some of his thoughts were quite profound.

One Spring I called on him and he was digging ground ready for planting potatoes. Usually Bob was reasonably polished in his speaking but when in conversation with another countryman he slipped into the local dialect. "How doo- How bee," he said in greeting. "OK thanks" I replied, already finding it difficult not to revert to my native tongue by saying" Vine, thankee." After a few minutes talking about the weather and the family, Bob turned to the barking dog which was penned in a large cage adjacent to the garden. "Will you be quiet Judy vor pity's sake." "That dog can't understand why I be digging this ground today, I reckon he's thinking how daft I be. Last Zaturday we went out rabbiting, in fact we were out rabbiting this last dree wicks. They are a real terrible pest at the present. Farmer Marlow was more than pleased for we bagged a couple dozen last wick." The dog barked again, "See," says Bob, "that dog reckons that I be stupid. Tis a lovely day and here I am making myself hot and bothered, wearing myself out digging this heavy clay soil when we could be out in the field or copse scurrying after rabbits and having a fine old time. 'Tis like this see, she's a dog and she don't understand why I be digging ere. All she knows is the fun of rabbiting." With a twinkle in his eye he continues: "I know that if I don't get these tators in we might starve next winter so even though I would like to go out rabbiting with her, I have got to stick to it. She only sees one side of it and nothing else."Bob stopped for the first time, pushed back his cap and scratched his head. Looking at me he said, "I reckon it's just like that with Him up there. We do fret and go because things don't happen as we want them to. I reckon He looks down on us just as I was looking at that dog just now. I reckon He feels sorry for us and says to himself, 'If only they could see the whole picture they'd know that all would work out for the best to them that love God'. "That's what the good book says, dun it?"

Time was going and Bob began digging again a little faster as if to make up for lost time. "That's right Bob," I said to myself as I went on my way, "your dad wasn't the only preacher in your family, was he? *

(A little while after this episode I married Bob Read's daughter, Margaret)

44

Are we Improving?

One morning, the birds were singing, dew- covered cobwebs on the shrubs glistened and sparkled in the bright rising sun and the atmosphere was fresh and clear. It was great to be alive. I picked up the paper and read of the magnificent response to the Children in Need appeal and the notion came to me that perhaps society is improving and slowly getting better with regard to its concern for others.

Not long ago a shop in my local town changed hands. It had been a hardware business for over 160 years. At one time it was very important, employing many people, but had become run down in latter years with only one of the family left, who, completely alone, served in the shop.

The charm of this place was that there had been very few alterations for perhaps a hundred years so it was like a 'time warp'. The shop was quaint yet it was the office at the back that enthralled me. The desks were at standing height, surrounded by archaic ledgers, but it was the notice by the door that shocked me. Boldly in capitals, was hand painted: IN CASE OF FIRE FIRST RESCUE THE SHOP BOOK. How about the dozen apprentices on the third floor with very steep steps to descend? I know that the owners of this business were upright Christian men, considered to be exemplary employers. As the last owner explained, "Of course the staff would have been alerted, that didn't need to be said, but one thing was certain, that precious shop book on which the future of the business depended would not walk out on its own."

Can you imagine, however, a notice being posted up in a modern business requesting that the computer disks should be rescued first? It wouldn't happen, for safety at work is paramount now so perhaps our sense of values has improved over the years. As I said, I was thinking about this one sunny morning and then I continued to read the newspaper. Fighting in Bosnia - Increase in Crime - Immorality in high places - Child Abuse and so it went on.

Despite some very welcome expressions of love, the human

race is just as capable of gross depravity as ever. My beautiful morning is clouding over - or is there an answer?

I'll go for the only one that has ever made sense to me. The hearts of people need to be changed. Fear, power, coercion has never achieved this, but a God who loves and continues to love has, and He can change not only the most depraved of individuals but also those of us who know that we could be better. *

Intruding Thoughts

My wife thinks I have an over-active mind. No, she doesn't think that I'm clever - it's just that my mind is always running off at a tangent. We are talking about a subject and the conversation reminds me of something else. Before I know what is happening I'm so engrossed in this new line of thought that I have forgotten the conversation which started it. "You don't hear a thing I say," she says as I grope for just a mere trifle to remind me what it was all about.

I know I have this failing, but my most creative ideas and inspirations have come to me when I should be concentrating on other things. Take last Sunday at church for instance. The preacher asked before the service started if there was any one for whom we should be praying. Immediately there leapt to my mind a dear friend who was about to enter hospital for a liver transplant. I was bold enough to mention his name and other names were added. The prayer began and the minister mentioned something which fired my imagination and I was away! The prayer came to an end and we were halfway through the Lord's prayer when I came to myself, "But I didn't pray for Richway. Better do it now." So I hastily phrased a silent prayer for the persons who had been mentioned. At the same time I asked God to forgive me for my lapse of concentration.

I was reminded at that moment of a story I heard years ago of a preacher who, during the prayer, suddenly remembered that he hadn't put the brake on in his car. Desperate to know whether the car had rolled down the hill, he suggested that the congregation should continue for a few moments in silent prayer. He quickly left the church through the vestry door and was relieved to find the car where he had parked it. He got inside to check the brake but before he realised it, the familiar feel of the seat and the steering wheel in his hand was persuasive to him driving off, which he promptly did leaving an incredulous congregation in silent prayer. Who thought up this unlikely story I don't know, but it caused me to smile.

Oh, Lord, I've done it again for our preacher is half way through the first reading now! "Oh God, what can I do to hold my concentration for the matter in hand?"

It seemed as though I heard him say, "I know all about it my son, and I understand. Why don't you present your intruding thoughts to me as well and make them part of your worship. After all they are about life and I'm interested in all of life."

I had never thought of it like that before and asked Him to accept my stray thoughts, funny story and all. It seemed as though by doing this I was closer to Him.

The time for communion arrived and I prayed, "Don't let any distractions come between us now, Lord." I took the bread and the wine and for those brief moments my mind was focused on a Saviour whose love was so great that he was prepared to die for all; the single minded mystic, the penitent murderer and the many like myself who so desperately want to give Him undivided attention but continually see His world breaking through.

The Desire to Belong

My wife and I have recently renewed our interest in genealogy. As both our families have lived for generations within five miles radius of where we live now, you can guess that we have discovered some interesting facts. We have found more relatives amongst our neighbours and have come across more than one 'skeleton in the cupboard'. Researching our family history has become an interesting hobby but was our interest sparked off by deeper emotions?

Recently I was listening to a broadcast (on the BBC World Service) in which they suggested that the increasing interest that people were taking in their family history was proportional to the break up of everyday family life. They cited an underground vault in Paris where family records are stored. Twenty years ago it was visited by a handful of people but now it is packed with researchers.

The broadcast cited some possible causes like the increase in the divorce rate, one-parent families and the receding influence of the church. Other possible reasons could be the emancipation of women and the general migration of children from the community where they were born. Folk are becoming more and more isolated yet inside they have this strong desire to belong.

Our interest in genealogy has been spasmodic over many years, but it is true to say that now our circumstances have changed. Our children are married and live miles away. From having an extended family of eight living in our village 12 years ago, we now have only one, so is there some deep emotional insecurity which has prompted our search?

Some years ago I went for a Youth Leaders' Weekend course and recall one activity particularly. The assembly of about 50, who were mostly unknown to each other, was asked to get blindfolded and to wander around the hall until they received further instructions. To begin with it was a joke. We bumped into each other and would laugh and have a conversation; however, as time went on we began to ask each other questions. "Do you know what's happening?" "What's it all about?" After a quarter of an hour, some were becoming quite disturbed at not knowing its purpose. One woman asked if she could hold on to my arm as she was becoming frightened. After 20 minutes the leader spoke to a now rather subdued group. "Blindfolds off," he said. The revealing fact was that all of us had formed ourselves into little motionless huddles. There wasn't a one solitary person on the floor. The leader then said, "You have learnt an important point this evening: the fact that human beings don't like to be isolated, they need other people, they need to belong."

True unconditional friendship may not be a perfect substitution for family but often it does restore into individuals the feeling of bonding and kinship. For this reason there is a growing need for people to make friends.

Think for a moment also of the many people forced into total isolation. Some have only retained their sanity by remembering continually their family and friends. Many also have been comforted by their belief that they not only belonged to God but that he was there, at their side, suffering as well.*

Imagination

I was driving a campervan along the suburbs of a local town. As I turned into a road, I noticed that it was called the Runway. Then I remembered that, during the war, this area now covered with houses had been an airfield. It was only a road sign but it had propelled me into a fantasy world. As I drove down this road, my cab became a cockpit as I imagined myself in a Spitfire rolling down this flat expanse prior to take off. Of course it was only in a moment of time because the surrounding traffic soon brought me down to earth. It has happened to me before when I have driven on the straight road across the Forest which used to be the railway line. I could almost smell the smoke as I was transported in my imagination onto the blackened, greasy and hot footplate of a puffing locomotive of a bygone day.

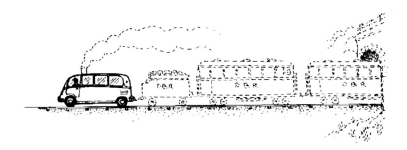

The imagination has such a powerful influence on us and upon it the natural development of children depends. "Drive a bit faster, Daddy," the kids shouted as, years ago, we drove down a long straight piece of road with a series of small hills on it. We called it the switchbacks and our children always elected to return home by this route which was so evocative of the fairground. Often we speak down to a child who is fantasising by saying, "You've got too vivid an imagination".

I remember reading once that if the imagination and the will had a battle the imagination invariably wins. I am sure there is a lot of truth in this. If you enter into a project with the imagined belief that it's going to be a failure, I'm sure that you are halfway towards it's sad demise.

The lesson is that we should try and be positive in our thinking, always trying to imagine success and reluctant to contemplate failure.

Occasionally I have had people say to me, "I would do anything to have a faith, but I simply can't believe." "I'm a realist", they say, "my intellect just won't let me believe that God became man and that his death two thousand years ago can be in any way relevant to me now." I don't argue or try to convince I simply say, "If you really would do anything for a faith why don't you just try and imagine that the claims of Christ are true? Pretend if you like, act as though what He said is true and that He is with you and cares for you". In a sense, should they take me up by imagining like this, they will have already made the first step of faith. They have said, "I want to know you, Lord, and I'm going to imagine you are real until I do know you." It's worth trying, for it could add a whole new meaning to life, bring untold happiness and hope for eternity.*

Amazing Grace

Our family had not long arrived at the campsite . The tent was erected and we were making our first cup of tea, having driven down to a site near Arcachon on the West Coast of France. Suddenly a distressed young woman appeared at the opening and looked at us with appealing eyes. "Please," she said, "could you lend me ten pounds. I've lost my purse and am now penniless. My husband is coming tomorrow and I just want something to tide me over. You are the only other English people here and I do hope you can help me." I suppose in those days ten pounds was half a week's wage and we couldn't afford to lose it. Already we had "pushed the boat out" just getting there. There was no way of checking her honesty. What were we to do? We couldn't send her away empty-handed but would she pay us back? I then noticed her wrist watch. "Why not leave your watch with me as security and we will lend you ten pounds," I said. Reluctantly she agreed and we felt that we had done the best we could under the circumstances.

The next day she returned and almost threw the ten pounds at us as she harshly asked for her watch. As my wife produced it, she snatched it from her and walked away not even saying thank you, obviously annoyed that her compatriots hadn't trusted her.

Why is it that some twenty five years later I still regret not giving her the money unconditionally? Why do I feel so guilty for not trusting her? Others have tried to console me. "There are thousands of people who have been duped and regretted it. You ought to be thankful you didn't lose your ten pounds," they say. Somehow I can't get it out of my mind that what I did was so "safe". Anyone would do it, even a member of the Mafia! As a Christian I should have gone the extra mile, taking a risk, and helped the distressed person because I cared and felt for her.

In the Sermon on the Mount Jesus says our love for others should be extraordinary. "There must be no limits to your goodness," he says, "as your heavenly Father's goodness knows no bounds." The one thing which gives me reassurance is that the God in whom I believe took such risks for me. He laid his life right on the line for my benefit. For many Christians, despite trying and having a deep commitment, they become increasingly aware of their failures. Their only consolation is that He has offered them undeserved, unlimited credit in terms of love and forgiveness. They call it Grace. Amazing Grace.*

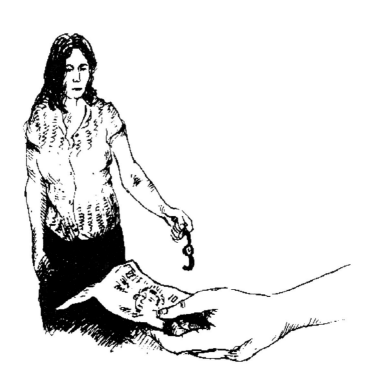

Too Close

Living near to the chalk hills of Wiltshire, Dorset and Hampshire we are familiar with seeing the various emblems carved out of the turf and which from a distance show up distinctly as a horse, a badge or a man. Some of them are thousand of years old and must have been significant visual displays for the people of that age.

It was only just recently that I actually walked on one of these, the White Horse at Westbury, which has now been given a permanent cement cover. What surprised me was that if anyone had asked me what the figure was I was standing on, I would have been hard put to say if I hadn't known before. I was too close to see.

I recall some years ago in a church youth club one or two of the girls had a crush on the youth leader. Many in the church could see this and thought that he should be careful, as it could become a problem. When told about this, the young man was quite oblivious to the attention being paid to him and thought his advisers were imagining it. Their reply was, "You can't see the wood for the trees." He was too close to the situation.

Sometimes I think people get too close to the Bible and by taking a text here and a phrase there and putting them together out of context produce some extraordinary concepts, quite out of keeping with the overall message of the book. This has sometimes resulted in the formation of a new sect.

There are also mistranslations and some apparent contradictions, which by just looking too closely could cause confusion, and in some cases genuine heartache for some trying to square it all up.

I remember hearing someone say once that the Bible was like a painting, a masterpiece. If you look at it very closely you see all the brush marks and smudges and if you look at it with a magnifying glass you will even see the texture of the canvas background. But if you were to stand back you would see a glorious picture of a benevolent God as shown in Jesus. Its overall impression is one of warmth, love and cheer because it speaks of hope.

One text gets near to expressing this overall picture and is found in St John's Gospel: "God so loved the world, that he gave his only begotten Son that whosoever believes in Him should not perish but have everlasting life."

Jesus himself recognised that people could look too closely at the scriptures and by emphasising the detail could lose the spirit. Once he healed a girl on the Sabbath day, which enraged the strict Jewish officials who said it was against the teaching of Moses. Jesus reproved them by saying. "Hypocrites! You would rescue one of your animals if it fell into the ditch on the Sabbath but you wouldn't help this unhappy woman."

He was equally pertinent talking about how they should be careful not to judge people. "Don't look for the speck of sawdust in someone else's eye when you have a plank of wood sticking out of your own," He said. Come to think of it, you can't get very close to another with such an encumbrance, can you? *

Face Value

When at school there was one girl who I thought was ugly. My mother scolded me when I told her. "No one is ugly," she said. "There's something beautiful about everyone." She hadn't convinced me. I'm sure this girl knew how unattractive she was because her behaviour reflected her looks. As she became a teenager a remarkable thing happened. Her skinny appearance rounded and her face became fuller. Her mouth, which once seemed to be too big, now emphasised her lovely teeth and the high cheekbones showed just enough to make her look distinctive from others. In fact she developed into a striking, eye-catching young lady. I wondered if her childhood years had been blighted by the reaction of her playmates at school.

Some years ago a representative called into the shop to sell me his wares. What my reaction was when I looked up I don't know, for this man had suffered horrific burns all over his face. The muscles had been affected too and the skin seemed wooden and unreal. He introduced himself and I gave him an initial order. I found as months went by that I was ordering because I felt sorry for him. One day he confronted me with this: "I know you have been ordering from me out of sympathy. I don't want that. If I am to succeed I want genuine orders." From then onwards we became good friends and I can honestly say a time came when I didn't notice his disfigurement. His personality shone through and I liked him. I recall taking him out for coffee and wondering why people were staring at us.

To a person who has a disfigurement, it must sound heartless to say that ultimately looks are not the most important thing one possesses, yet deep down we know it is true. All of us have known people to whom initially we took a dislike because we didn't like their appearance but have later found them to be delightful. The notion has become part of the English language. Never accept things at "face value" we say. I know it's not much consolation to the sufferer but it is true. Everyone would prefer an unattractive person with a good nature to a pretty but nasty individual. So why do we get so hung up on looks? Why must we have this obsession with appearances, or is it we are we just being got at by the "glossies" and advertising gurus?

I'm glad that there are good grounds for not taking things at face value. In the Old Testament we find many sentences which shine like perpetual beacons and one particularly reveals to me an understanding of God which later was summed up in the life of Jesus.

"The Lord does not see as man sees; men judge by appearances but the Lord judges by the heart." *

The Romany

I must confess I overstepped the mark the other day. A gypsy encampment had appeared on the village common. A colourful traditional caravan with the horse quietly nibbling grass while a man sat by his fire, from which a wisp of grey smoke curled up against a background of green, flowering maythorn.

I went to video the general scene determined that I would not intrude by taking close-ups. In my viewfinder I could see the gypsy move. He was coming in my direction. I greeted him with a cheery "Good Morning." "Why didn't you ask my permission to film me?" he said politely. I felt uncomfortable but tried to defend myself by saying that I didn't think I needed permission to film my own common, especially as he was only a small part of the general scene. "You wouldn't like me to film your house without permission," he said. "I would feel honoured if you took a picture of the outside of my house," I retorted. So started a civilised conversation when I was able to tell him that before the war the gypsy families would come, and for the short time they were there they would become integrated into the village. They would come to Sunday School and would be invited to the Christmas party.

He told me how he was harassed and abused, accused wrongly of living on the state, of not paying taxes, and of being chased from pillar to post.
I was able to explain to him why his presence did threaten some people in the village. Whereas they might not be against a visit of a single caravan occasionally, they were afraid that this might be a trigger for many to descend on the common. What about the toilet facilities and public health? Some might not be so considerate as him and play loud music continually. Supposing they were joined by "junkies" or "ravers", and what would it do to the condition of the common where children played, not to mention the effect it might have on property values?

After talking for some while we had become friends and I apologized for not asking his permission and would, after showing him the video, wipe it off in his presence. "No, don't do that," he said. "You put it with your records of the village and then if in future years anyone wants proof that we camped here, you've got it!"

Gypsies are God's children, too. Surely there must be some way we can, with safeguards, accommodate their culture into our system. After all, Jesus himself was a bit of a Gypsy, too. A roaming preacher who was sometimes driven from village to village and often had "nowhere to lay his head".*

Relativity

According to a recent report, exploration into the mysteries of the universe using the latest outer space radio probes and the Hubble satellite telescope have found nothing which would disprove Einstein's theory of relativity. In 1905 this brilliant thinker had come up with a new way of regarding the relationship of Time, Space, Matter and Energy. His theory has led to the advances in the control of atomic energy and to some of the current investigations into space.

I hope you will not think me presumptuous but I have come up with another theory of Relativity. The exact formula I am not clever enough to work out but I can tell you the constants. They are Judgement, Knowledge, Circumstance and Experience ie. J.KC.E.

Let me explain. When I regard any item of news, my judgement is affected by my knowledge, my present circumstances and my experience. J.K.C.E. Recently there was an account of the deprivation of many poor people in China. I had just returned from a visit to that beautiful country and had witnessed begging on the streets. Because I enjoy the affluence of the west, my perspective of that report will be entirely different from that of a lad sleeping rough in one of our cities who is perpetually hungry and can hardly remember the last time he slept in comfort.

Years ago I recall being scolded by my wife's grandmother because I had highlighted some minor indiscretion of an upright and honourable resident of our village. "Just one minute," she said "I want to tell you something." She then went on to relate the dreadful upbringing this person had experienced by a cruel father who was constantly under the influence of drink. "Often," she said, "the poor boy instead of going to school would be dragged off to do the work which his father would be too drunk to do. When I see him now and think of what he might have become but for the grace of God, I can only rejoice." Suitably admonished, I saw that man in a new light from then onwards.

The perplexing question is: How then can we know what is

truth if every judgement is coloured as my theory would suggest? I think our only hope is to endeavour to put ourselves into the circumstances and experience of others and try and forget our own position. I suppose you could call it involvement. The coming of God into the world in Jesus, to share in the human experience, can partly be explained in that he wanted to know just what our lot was like. Similarly His followers in every generation have given up peace, tranquillity and safety so that they could enter into the daily existence of others and be able to help because they shared their experience.

So, with apologies to Albert Einstein, I would claim my theory on Relativity is an important factor of life and those who wish to be realistic and objective in their observations must always take it into account. *

Politically Correct

The other day I was rebuked for calling a woman a lady. I was relating to a friend my conversations with a woman I had encountered and simply said, "I met this lady down the street." Before I could go any further my friend interrupted and said, "Woman, if you don't mind. To call a female a lady is demeaning and condescending so don't use that term when speaking to me." I was taken aback as it is as much part of my vocabulary as gentleman or child. I was told that it is not now politically correct.

I thought she was over-reacting but it did serve to make me more sensitive to the feelings of others. Of course, many words that have acquired such loathsome historical significance one would not dream of using today. To do so would be at the least unkind and at worst could be considered an incitement to violence. However I do wonder whether perhaps sensitivity for the feelings of others sometimes goes a bit too far.

The definition of 'Political Correctness' is that one should not say or do anything which might cause offence to others. To what extremes do you take this? Many of the great reforms in society came about because there were people of the day who were prepared to cause offence to a substantial number of people.

Whether it was William Wilberforce and his outspoken words against slavery or Pastor Martin Niemöller who, during the War, was prepared to speak out boldly in Berlin about his deep dislike of the Nazis' activities - both broke the law of political correctness of their day but who would dispute their actions now?

Recently I heard of a brave lady (sorry, woman,) who stood up for what she believed, despite a peculiar twist in political correctness. It was her first day as a secretary to a formidable boss and immediately, because of his bad language, she knew she would be unhappy. The other staff didn't seem to mind but she decided she would have to tell him of her distress. In one age it would have been considered politically incorrect to swear in front of the female sex but in these days of equality she supposed that that particular convention had been swept away and that she was treading on dangerous ground. "Ex-c-cuse me," she said timidly "but I wonder if you would refrain from s-swearing in my presence please. You use the name of my God profanely and every time you do, it p-pains me." She watched his colour rise. His face became slightly contorted and she thought he was going to burst into a rage. Looking straight at her he said quietly, "Of course I will. I'm so sorry." She continued to work happily for him for a considerable time.

So I think of political correctness as a valuable reminder that we should be generally kind and considerate to the feelings of others but if the occasion arose when to be true to our conscience it was necessary to cause offence to others, I hope that some of us would have the courage to speak out.*

"I've got to tell somebody"

The young people in our church made a video of the parable told by Jesus of the woman who lost and found her precious coin. It was a modern version of the story and they made up the words as the story went along. I recall Rebecca, who took the lead role, bursting excitedly out of the bedroom after finding the coin saying as she lifted the telephone, "I've got to tell somebody." I was reminded of this when I was doing some research at the County Record Office. I was sitting in front of a microfiche reader along with a row of other researchers. Suddenly a sophisticated young lady sitting next to me became excited and nudged me. "Look," she said, "I've found it! I've been looking for this information for years." Then suddenly realising she was talking to a stranger she regained her composure. "I'm sorry," she said, "but I had to tell somebody."

Anyone who has lost some one dear to them will know that one of the things they miss most is the sharing of news and experiences. One friend recently widowed told me, "I go out shopping and I see that a friend has had a new baby or a new store has opened and I say to myself, 'I must remember to tell Norman about that,' and then it dawns on me that Norman won't be home when I return."

When I was about twelve I was, for my age, quite clever with wireless sets. In our hamlet people would ask me to call and repair them when they went wrong. I recall once being asked to mend the Revd. West's old valve radio at The Manse. I managed to get it going and from the speaker there came the most beautiful music I had ever heard. As I listened I knew I had to share it with my dad who was the church organist and keen on classical music. Asking the Reverend to excuse me, I rushed out of the house and bounded down the hill. "Dad! Quick! Switch on the Home Service. I want you to hear some beautiful music." Together we sat and listened to the remainder of Nimrod from Elgar's Enigma Variations. It was a magic moment when a son got so much pleasure sharing something special with his dad. It's always been the same; humans just can't keep good things to themselves.

The last words of Jesus before his Ascension were to command his followers to proclaim the Good News about him throughout the world. I reckon the reason it spread so effectively was not just because of Christ's command but because Christians were bubbling over with happiness. Christ had made such a difference to their lives that they simply had to tell others about him.*

Bookseller?

Some memories return with great delight as you relive happy experiences and often they remain with you for days, adding a bounce to your feet and a lilt of gladness to your speech. The other day I woke up and a memory came back to me which had the reverse effect. I was incensed because of the injustice meted out to me some 57 years ago and which was never put right.

The situation was the classroom of a village school and the subject was English. The teacher asked the question, "If a butcher is the seller of meat what do you call a man who sells books?" I knew it and put my hand up, willing her to ask me for the answer. She pointed at me so my moment had come. "A colporteur, Miss." "A colporteur?" she said sardonically. "Don't be so foolish." I recall the sarcasm as she said, "Sit down, little man. You tell him, Sidney. What is the name of a man who sells books?" "A bookseller, Miss". All the children laughed and I was crest-fallen and here I am after all these years still suffering the grievance. Perhaps telling you will get it out of my system.

"Just one minute," I can hear you say, "but what is a colporteur? I've never heard of the name." I can tell you now, as I did then, that a colporteur _is_ the seller of books, for he visited my country home, every month opened a case and sold some to my mother. Incidentally he also sold her writing paper and other items of stationery. During the war he served a real need in isolated communities, especially as my mother used to send frequent letters to my father who was away working on munitions. We children looked forward to getting storybooks and the colporteur, a friendly man called Mr. Jarvis, after opening his case would often give us a sweet. Let me tell you the definition of a colporteur: a book-peddler, especially employed by a society to sell Bibles. Mr. Jarvis was a traveller for the Spurgeons Colportage Association, a society set up to distribute Bibles and wholesome books. This association certainly met the need of the age and conveyed the Good News of Jesus not only by literature but also by the regular visits

67

of the colporteur who recognised the spiritual and social needs of isolated folk, where often the nearest telephone was several miles away.

We have entered the era of communicating the Gospel by CD Rom, The Internet and other emerging media developments which, of course, is right for our age; but I wonder if anything can really replace the personal visit of someone like the friendly and helpful colporteur of my youth.

By the way, if there are some teachers listening. I suggest that if a child answers your question in an odd way don't brush him aside. He just might be right. *

"I'm Angry"

Usually my thoughts are cheerful and uplifting but tonight they express resentment. I'm angry because I see beautiful children, healthy, well fed, well clothed but deprived. They are deprived of people around them behaving naturally for now many decent, normal adults tend to treat children as a forbidden area, only to be talked to when there's someone about.

Shortly before I retired I had to call on a customer and attend to his video recorder. The system had to be set up again. I knelt down in front of the set and proceeded to press the appropriate buttons. No sooner had I started than Jamie, the four-year old son of the family, knelt down close to me watching my every movement and the various menus and pictures which came onto the screen. I can only think that perhaps my jacket sleeve floated across his head or arm as I moved forward to press yet another button. It was then the little boy looked up and said, "Mr. Bailey, don't tickle me". The effect on me was electric. My face went red as I quickly looked round to see if anyone had heard in case they misconstrued his remark. "Go and see what mummy's doing," I said. The boy scrambled up and ran into the kitchen. I was so glad that no one had heard the innocent remark but intensely angry that he had been deprived of satisfying his natural curiosity and I had been deprived of the joy of relating to a child.

A friend of ours has for years helped care for the infants in a local Sunday School. She was the extra helper who took them to the toilet, nursed them if they fell, wiped their tears away and generally cared for them. She told me recently that she had finished doing this service because if she continued she would have to be registered as a helper. "I don't feel like going through this now," she said. So the children are deprived of a "grandmother" figure whom they greatly loved. Voluntary workers with children have to follow a code of practice and have to be registered. Of course, I know it is necessary. There is no other way to protect our children but that doesn't stop me from being angry. Because of the actions of relatively few child abusers, all children are deprived not only of the freedom to play in the streets but also of being treated naturally by adults.

Whenever I say in The Lord's Prayer "Thy Kingdom come," I think of a time when the climate of behaviour is such that children can roam the streets without fear, and adults can cuddle a child without feeling they might be labelled a pervert.

It may be pictorial language but surely the prophet in the Bible was imagining such a day when he said ' The lion shall lie down with the lamb and a little child shall lead them'. *

The Chapel down the Hill

For the past 48 years I have lived in the village of Sandle-heath, Hampshire and have been involved with the small Methodist chapel there. In that time there have been many changes as I have watched two generations of Godly men and women faithfully worship and serve in "this chapel down the hill".

One of the most dramatic changes was in the early 70's when the Church Council unanimously decided to have the church gutted, turned round and completely revamped. Part of this exercise included the removing the of the old porch and building a vestry on the front. Unfortunately, some of the dedication stones laid by the faithful of past years had to be removed and relaid in the wall of the vestry. I recall one of the old stalwarts complaining that our church was telling a lie because the stone which said "This stone was laid by Sidney Beckingham" was actually laid by a brickie of the builders Wayman and Sons!

I was erecting a Christmas tree on the vestry roof recently and had to place the ladder against the wall. Thinking of my old friend's comment, I smiled to myself as I read the names once more but it set me thinking again of the history of the place.

On its fiftieth anniversary a newspaper report says that an account of the history of the church given by a certain George Witt was a "pleasing feature". Of course his talk was not recorded but with some research through family records I have produced the following.

The Primitive Methodist Magazine of February 1845 relates how, after a series of camp meetings on the common by visiting preachers and subsequent regular meetings in a small cottage, a "movable church" was built here. It was only twenty four feet by fifteen feet in size housing two pews and "eight sittings with railed backs". It appears that the place was supported by a lady of substance, a certain Lady Warmington. As the century progressed it would seem that interest waned, the faithful

71

died and the cause was almost if not completely abandoned. It was reported that "there was but one praying person" for which I suppose we should be profoundly grateful, for those prayers were answered in a strange way. The story goes that in about 1881 four teenagers including George Witt were soundly converted whilst working with a certain George Stainer and William Hammond, "illiterate but prayerful men". These young men looked out to find what God wanted them to do. At first they attended Rockbourne Baptist Chapel and were greatly encouraged by a devout local preacher from Damerham, William Ambrose. It was not long before they became aware of the floundering (or floundered) cause at Sandleheath. They set out on Sunday afternoons, visited the people of this rural industrial village, which boasted five brickyards, and held open air meetings. As a result many responded to the call of Christ and became committed Christians. The cause took on a new lease of life and it wasn't long before they were looking for a site on which to build a larger church. The local Methodist Circuit, ministers and leaders were not at all enthusiastic about embarking on such an ambitious proposal and turned them down. I suppose they were entitled to be cautious for after all the prime movers were under twenty years of age and could they be relied upon to fulfil the financial liability? The Circuit certainly did not want to be left with an outstanding debt should their enthusiasm wane. Undaunted, the young men persisted in their request and eventually they received the Circuit's permission and blessing. In 1884 the first piece of land was bought and the first part of our present building was erected and opened in 1884 at a cost of £140.

As I said, looking at the dedication stones placed in the new wall started me thinking about the past and our wonderful heritage. What of the future? Who can say where God is leading us? I know that we are in good heart and that our church building is in good structural repair. At present we enjoy good relations with our Anglican friends in the village with whom we hold monthly united services and combine for social activities. I pray that, whatever happens, the witness of Christ in this community will continue.

Inspired by Friends

HILDA WHITLOCK

Ralph Whitlock, broadcaster and writer, might not now be a name known in every household but for a generation of youngsters in the 50s he was famous. Ralph was the author who also acted the part of Farmer Whitlock in the Children's Hour series "A Visit to Cowleaze Farm". He was a prolific writer of books about the countryside and he also had many admirers of his regular columns in newspapers and magazines. But I want to talk about his greatest fan and helpmate, Hilda, his devoted wife who had faithfully supported him throughout his interesting and varied career.

Ralph came home one day in 1983 to find that Hilda had collapsed. For several weeks she was in a coma hovering between life and death, but following major surgery she returned home paralysed, partially blind and confused. It was more than a year before she began to respond to intensive therapy though little hope was given for her complete recovery. However, with the prayers and support of Ralph, her family, friends and therapists, she began to make some progress. When a girl, Hilda had played the organ at the village chapel. The young Ralph was regularly in the congregation. When they had retired and had returned to the village, she had again taken up the role. During therapy one of the sisters asked her what her hobbies were and she replied: "Playing the organ." "You may as well put that out of your head," was the reply, "you will never play the organ again." This was just the incentive Hilda needed, for she began some self-induced therapy to get those immobile fingers moving. She struggled relentlessly to free the static limbs and bring life back to inactive joints. Often disappointed and frustrated, she fought to touch the right notes on the organ, watched over by a helpless but sympathetic husband. Gradually Ralph noticed that the music emerging from the organ was becoming more melodious and almost imperceptibly Hilda's attempts at playing were more relaxed. Four years after her stroke Hilda was playing the chapel organ again every Sunday. The local paper called her the Miracle Woman.

As a thanksgiving for her remarkable healing, at the age of 72, Hilda played an all-day organ marathon in the village chapel to raise money for charity, and she repeated it last year on her eightieth birthday.

Later that year Ralph died and some wondered who should be asked to play the organ at the funeral, but they needn't have worried for Hilda had already made up her mind. "I will play," she said, "it's what Ralph would have wanted." So though of course people were sad because of Ralph's passing, it was also a time of celebration not only of a life well lived, but of human love and of triumph over disaster. *

(Hilda died in 2001 and was still playing the organ within the last few months of her life.)

Inspired by Friends

A Happy Happening

An article in a newspaper recently made me ask myself the question: "What event has given me real happiness?" Directly a scene came to my mind which still gives me pleasure when I think of it.

In our town up to a few years ago we had a saddler. This business fascinated me as the owner and his son were craftsmen of the old school. If a job was worth doing it was worth doing well regardless of the time taken. Mr West sat on his stool in the corner sewing a harness by hand, whilst his son was using a sewing machine to repair a briefcase or a bag.

One day I walked in and Mr West wasn't working. He looked dejected and utterly miserable. "It had to come," I thought to myself. "He must be eighty. It's time he thought about retiring." Charlie must have read my thoughts. "Dad's a bit low today," he said. "He can't see to work any more. He's got cataracts in both eyes. Of course, for sewing you've got to have good sight." One day I called in and he wasn't there. "Dad's gone to have the operation to remove the cataracts from his eyes," he said. "Let's hope and pray that it's successful," I replied.

A few weeks later I breezed into the shop. Everything was so normal that for a moment I had forgotten - then it dawned on me. There was Mr. West, in his usual corner sewing again and looking as happy and excited as if he'd just begun his first day at work. "I'm glad to see you back working again," I said. A man of few words he just said, "You're not half as glad as I am."

It wasn't long before Mr West died, and no doubt some might argue that his operation was a waste of resources and the money should have been spent on someone more likely to be able to enjoy its benefit longer.

I don't view it in that way. Just to see this old man enjoying life again provided me with one of my most memorable happy experiences. When the people brought the sick folk to Jesus, you can't imagine Him turning some away because they were old.

Yet doctors do often face such a dilemma and need our support in obtaining more resources. This also means joining with those who seek to use more effectively the funds available and making sure that by an unhealthy life style we don't fill those precious beds unnecessarily.

Happiness is priceless and has a knock on effect. Mr. West's elation had rubbed off on many who had witnessed a miracle. Who can say what effect this uplifting joy had made on the lives of others? It might even have saved the NHS money! *

Who's to Say?

Alec Butler was a character. He was a farmer who had the reputation of being comical. It was his wife who kept the farm going through out their long but happy married life. It was she who made sure Alec got up in the mornings, for he was as alive as a cricket at midnight but at the beginning of the day he was good for nothing. It is reputed that he bought a donkey at the market and because his wife was ill in bed, he took it upstairs to show her!

I know for a fact that he called at the local brickworks and was full of his usual nonsense. He ended up with these words which have passed down through our family and are often quoted when one of us does something which might be called eccentric. "You know, I can't make it out. Some people call me daft and I call other people daft. Who's to say who is daft?" (Or in dialect as Alec would have said it "Wast think, I can't meak it out, zum people call I daft, and I call tothers daft. Who'z to zay who is daft?")

Recently I visited a home and was impressed by two pictures on the wall. One was a drawing called Flight Delayed and depicted the various groups of people in an airport lounge. It was all there, the utter frustration, pent up anger and in some cases sheer resignation; parents trying to restrain their fractious children whilst one man is stretched out the full length of the settee, asleep.

The other picture is a painting of the lounge in an old people's home. Again it marvellously reflects the sadness, frustration, pain and dignity so often evident in such places.

Both pictures were the work of Miss Gardener, an old lady who used to talk to herself and was generally regarded as eccentric or senile. Some people, unkindly, said she was mad. She spent her final years in a retirement home and painting was a great therapy for her. Even then she had the perception, technique and inspiration to produce, to my mind, meaningful masterpieces. She was invited to the Christmas day dinner at a home where I was staying and I found her interesting and kindly. Although she did say one or two odd things, she was gracious in her attitude. It reminded me of Alec's comment: "Some call me daft and I call other people daft. Who's to say who is daft?" I've come to the conclusion that we are all too ready to make instant judgements and write people off perhaps because of their accent, colour, or unusual mannerisms. It does us good sometimes to look at ourselves and try to see what other people see in us. It can be very sobering.

It was Jesus who said that we shouldn't judge others or we risked being judged ourselves. He always saw the best in everyone and sought to uplift rather than condemn.

I'm just wondering what the comical Alec would say if he knew that his funny remark had initiated such a profound thought.

"You've had your Chips."

Mrs. Jaques was a lonely though lively old widow who lived near our home when I was a boy. During the war she often popped in for company and, like my mother, knitted gloves, which was a sort of cottage industry in those days. She suffered from an unfortunate tremor, but what amazed us was that despite the constant jog she could manipulate the needles and knit without looking at what she was doing. The sight of this lovely old lady jigging away at her knitting is still vivid in my mind now, some 60 years after. It has just come to me that she also had a large birthmark on her face, but her cheerful spirit and sense of fun made her disfigurement pale into insignificance.

One day she made the comment that Wilfred, a local hurdle maker, had not delivered her chips - the hazel off-cuts of wood with which she used to light her fire. My brother said to her, using a current expression, "Well that's too bad, Mrs. Jaques. It seems to me *you've had your chips*". "No," she said, "I've just told you that I haven't had my chips". Of course, we laughed and then tried to explain to her that it was an expression which meant that there wasn't much hope and that catch phrases mustn't be taken at "face value". She soon cottoned on and was using it on us in a few days!

Now that I'm older I'm having problems keeping up with the slang and sayings of today. For instance, enterprising businessmen have developed their own expressions. I discovered that a "no brainer" means that a project could be done *over and over again without extensive preparation.* Or that a "pay roll adjustment" meant *an employee would be fired and laid off* and a "boomranger" was *a young single person living with his parents.*

Some stories in the Bible should not be taken at face value either. Take for instance that strange story when Jesus seems to speak harshly to a foreigner who desperately wanted her child healed. "It isn't right to take the children's food and throw it to the dogs," he said. I puzzled over this seemingly racist remark for years. It seemed obvious that the "children" were the Jews and the "dogs" were the Gentiles. Such discrimination was so out of character to the Jesus I have come to know that I put it into a corner of my mind marked "waiting further illumination". Then I came across a reference to a commentary, which said that contemporary to the story, there was a popular proverb: "Children first - then the puppies." Perhaps this is the answer. Jesus was teasing her. With a twinkle in his eye he quotes the proverb. And she, seeing his smile, was quite unabashed and retorts with an equally outrageous suggestion: "But even the puppies eat the crumbs from under the table." And with that, commending the woman for her faith, he healed her child. I can't be sure that this is the explanation but it makes more sense to me. It's not unlike when the children kick the football into my garden and come to collect it. Teasing them I might say with a broad grin "Findzies Keepzies" but immediately hand them back the ball.

One thing I know - if we had been there during His lifetime, His smile and the catch phrases and colloquial expressions of the day would have added much to our understanding of His message.

Christmas

A Christmas Project

The run up to Christmas is certainly a hectic time. I'm almost worn out already. Never mind. I'm a bit earlier tonight. Might be able to put my feet up.

As I open the door, the arms of my four-year-old son are outstretched appealing for me to pick him up. Before I can kiss him, he is asking a question I have heard every night this week. "When are we going to start making the crib, Daddy?" I am wishing that I hadn't mentioned the fact that I had been asked to make the crib for the church nativity play. "Can we make it tonight, Daddy?" How he keeps on about it. I am tempted to suggest that we do it tomorrow, but those beautiful appealing blue eyes can be ignored no longer. "Right Alistair, we will do it now, before I have my meal, then you can go to bed."

First of all I must find some wood. There should be some in the shed. My excited son is waiting anxiously as I return with an old orange box, rather pleased that by using this the job is half done. With the "help" of little hands we soon have the box looking something like a crib. "Now you hold on to the wood whilst Daddy hammers the legs on," I say, making sure that he feels really involved in the project. Now we only have to turn it over and hammer on the other pair of legs and the job is done.

One little boy is happy and the crib is ready for Sunday week. I stand back to look at the finished job. It should look all right when filled with straw, I think to myself. Alistair is stroking it thoughtfully. "Something wrong, son?" I ask. He hesitates. Then, looking at the crib once again, he says, "Look. It's a bit rough, Daddy, isn't it?" I realise that he is not talking about my workmanship but the fact that the wood itself is rough and full of splinters. My mind however has taken another turn. Lifting him up, I begin to talk to him about a truth which is far too deep for him to understand. "Yes, Alistair. It is rough, and that's how it should be."

81

Despite the peace and homely charm of the Christmas card scene, showing the stable with clean wholesome straw, friendly, attentive animals and a serene, composed mother, the Christmas story was rough throughout. What about the filth, cold, smell and the damp one would expect in an eastern stable? How could a mother be expected to give birth to a healthy child under such dreadful conditions? "Yes, Alistair. I agree it is rough, and that's how it must be to remind us a little of what the Incarnation was really like." He struggles to get down, my murmuring having gone on too long. I lift up the crib, take it back to the shed and place it reverently down in the corner. As I stand back and look at it, I am reminded of the text we had heard at a service the previous Sunday. 'He was rich yet for our sakes he became poor so that through His poverty we might become rich.'

Alistair is now grown up and I have since been involved in many Nativity plays but a Christmas has not passed without my thinking of how my child's simple comment reminded me of the essential truth of the Incarnation.

(This was Broadcast on the BBC Radio 2 Pause for Thought programme on Christmas Day 1. 30 am and 3.30am 1994.)

Advent Candles

In our church, as in many others, we light a red candle each Sunday during Advent, the final candle, a single slender white decorative specimen representing Jesus, the Son of God, being lit at the Christmas Eve Communion Service.

At Christmas 1991 I was asked to provide the candles for Advent, which I dutifully did for four Sundays. On Christmas Eve I arrived home late from work, tired but glad that Christmas was actually here. Shortly before we were due to leave for the service, a cold sweat came over me. I had forgotten to get a white candle. What was I to do? My wife thought that there were some in the loft where, as an answer to my prayer, I found one solitary white candle in a box of red candles. However, my ecstasy suddenly turned to despair. It was broken in two places and was discoloured with red streaks along its side through its contact with the red candles.

"How can I use that?" I said to my wife. "It is supposed to be white and flawless, representing the perfect gift of God's Son." There was nothing for it - this broken candle would have to do. I tried to mend it by melting it over another candle, but the joints bulged with traces of black smoke, and, worst of all, the candle was not completely straight. However, this was the only one I had and perhaps at a distance it wouldn't show.

The Christmas Eve congregation were all busy munching their mince pies in the Church hall when we arrived. I crept into the Church and inserted the candle into the centre holder on the table. With a few pieces of holly, strategically placed, I was satisfied that the imperfections hardly showed.

Later, as I sat in the church enjoying the wonderful Christmas story told in readings and carols, I was gripped by that old Christmas magic of feeling good, that all was well. Peace on earth, goodwill to men. I had completely forgotten the feverish activity the past hour until the Minister lit the candle. The time has come to move forward to the communion rail to receive the sacrament.

As I kneel I take a tentative look at the candle my heart sinks. I notice that the candle from this angle looks misshapen and bent. How could I let myself tarnish this sacred act by being so casual? I bow my head and ask for forgiveness. The Minister is in front of me and, as I receive the bread, my now tearful eyes are drawn once again to the disfigured candle. The Minister whispers, "The Body of Christ which was broken for you." My blurred image of a bent candle changes to a broken man upon a cross. "The blood of Christ which was shed for you," the Minister murmurs as I receive the wine. Transfixed by the candle with the red streaks, I can only see the figure on a Cross - with blood streaming from His side.

The service is over. We all wish each other a happy Christmas but I am thinking of how my unworthy contribution to the service had at least conveyed to me the true meaning of Christmas; for in that baby of Bethlehem was enwrapped all the suffering and sins of the world.

(This was broadcast on the BBC Radio 2 programme on 18th Dec 1994 at 1.30 and 3.30 am)

A Non - Event?

The erection of the thirty five feet high Christmas tree in the centre of the market place has been a ritual I have been involved in for many years. My job has been to fit the festive lighting. Last year there was some confusion, which turned out to be a fiasco. On the morning when the erection was to take place every one was there: the JCB and its driver together with four hefty men with hard hats, a van with ladders, plus myself with strings of coloured bulbs. But where was the tree? Eventually it arrived but you can imagine our surprise and indignation for it was in total only twelve feet tall! One of the men carried it easily on his own and, to the amusement of the people in the bus queue, stuck it in the large hole intended for an enormous tree. The others left, leaving me to try to find a solution! I was subjected to light-hearted taunts and jibes which generally made the point that this was the biggest "non event" of the year. Everyone was there but the Christmas tree wasn't worth erecting. In fact another tree was obtained later in the day and honour was restored.

It set me thinking that Christmas itself is like this to some people. How many times have I been saddened when I've heard people say, "I shall be glad when it's all over". They have their families around them, they send and receive many cards and they give and accept choice presents. They put up expensive decorations and cook and eat a delicious Christmas dinner and afterwards say it wasn't worth the fuss. Some of us quarrel over the value of the presents we receive. Some of us eat or drink so much that we are really ill. Others are so overworked that the whole holiday is a slog. Christmas, the time of peace, happiness and good will passes us by. It's been a memorable 'non- event'.

Is there any remedy to this yearly endurance test? I believe there is and it's more to do with attitudes than material things. We have become so obsessed with possessions that we have missed the real message of the baby in Bethlehem.

One of the happiest Christmases I remember was as a boy in 1945. My sister, much to my disapproval, had become friendly with a German prisoner of war who was working on a local farm. She asked dad if he could spend Christmas with us. My parents said that in the circumstances they wouldn't enjoy their Christmas if he didn't come. "So I've got to accept a Hun sleeping in my bedroom, have I?" was my comment having, during my impressionable years, been subjected to all kinds of wartime propaganda. I was to learn a lot that Christmas. My hostility was replaced with love and understanding and when he eventually went back to Germany I was brokenhearted. The letters between them gradually declined and my sister fell in love with a super guy to whom she has been happily married for over 50 years. However I shall always remember how we made that Christmas a very happy time for a young soldier who was separated from his family and living in a hostile land. The amazing thing was that in our simple little country cottage with none of the modern amenities, we had something far more important. We had embraced the real message of the Christ child by showing love to another and received it back many times over. That was a truly happy Christmas and it's freely available this year to us all. *

Barn Social

The annual Church Christmas Social Evening has taken many different forms over the years. One year a farmer allowed us to use an ancient barn with a tall vaulted roof. It didn't cross our minds that it might be cold and that the barn would be difficult to heat. However, the planning went ahead and, as the time drew near, we swept it out and fitted up lights. It was then that we realised just how cold it was and made some very inadequate arrangements for heating, at the same time advertising to those wishing to attend to come well wrapped up. This social turned out to be a great success not least because of the temperature. Everyone took part in the games and square dances eagerly, just to keep warm. Whilst the handbell ringers played favourite carols, we warmed our hands on mugs of steaming hot soup.

We always ended our social with a short epilogue and I had planned that this time we would do a spontaneous Nativity play. I took a whole collection of drapes and costumes, which our teenagers could put over their clothes to portray the central characters. We asked for volunteers and such was the spirit of the occasion that immediately one said, "I'll be Joseph." Another said, "Can I be Mary?" and so on until all the parts had been filled. I had provided a crib so that the scene could be acted out on the floor of the barn but suddenly one voice said, "Why can't we do it over there?" pointing to a penned-off area at the end of the barn. I went to investigate and discovered that this area was used as a stable for the owner's ponies and, although it was only illuminated by the light from the main area, you could plainly see a manger full of hay fixed to the corner. The ponies were out in the paddock so I thought it would be suitable and safe to hold our Nativity play there. To the narration of the simple Bible story from the Gospels, the actors made their way across the rather unpleasant pungent straw and took their places just as they imagined they should. When the tableau was complete we all sang "Away in a Manger" and pondered over a particularly lovely though dimly-lit scene.

It was then something special happened which transformed the occasion. The two ponies approached the manger. Naturally the actors were anxious but none of them moved as one pony went right up to the manger and stayed there quietly as we finished the carol and said the grace. The actors and the ponies moved quietly away and all present had a feeling of elation. We felt we had shared in something special. The words of a carol came to me: "Cradled in a manger meanly lay the son of man his head". I don't think I had grasped just how mean it was until then. As one of the actors said to me, "I never realised before just how lowly the birth of Jesus was until those ponies moved in, their steaming breath encircling the manger. Oh, by the way, take a look at my trainers!"*

A Pondering "Preacher Man"

Called

The surroundings in which I was brought up were, to my mind, idyllic. The hamlet belonged to an estate adjacent to a large common. We were "free to roam" not by right but by favour because we "belonged". When I was six years old, war had called my father away to a Spitfire factory in Southampton. I missed him greatly but what with school, roaming, playing and tree-climbing the time between his leaves went quickly.

I had been brought up in a Christian home and don't remember any time when I wasn't aware of the love of God and the certainty of Jesus. There was no sudden experience but I do recall, as I became a teenager, being aware of the beauty, wonder and awesomeness of creation. I remember lying on the grass and looking up to the blue sky and thinking about infinity, of listening to the music of country sounds about me, birds singing in a thicket nearby, cows mooing as they made their way to the farm for milking, the rustling of the leaves as they moved in a gentle breeze and the sudden buzz of a bee or fly as it flew by, and thinking this world is wonderful and God made it.

The Congregational chapel was the centre of our hamlet, both physically and socially and everything that was of interest happened there. Every person there was a friend - many of whom, though unrelated, we called Aunty or Uncle.

When I was sixteen I was asked to be chairman at a Tuesday night meeting and had to do a short address. Looking back it seems pretentious that I should be talking to people so steeped in faith. Afterwards, I was commended for my short address and encouraged to do it again. Of course I made mistakes but I am sure that I was sincere and that I felt I did want to communicate the love of God as I knew it through my parents, and most of all by the person I had come to know as Jesus. The turning point came when a Mr. Castle from the little village of Godshill asked me to preach at the Congregational Chapel there. My dad asked me how I felt about it. I said that I thought I ought to accept, but

didn't know whether I was good enough. After prayerful considera-
tion, my feelings prompted me to accept the invitation. I was drawn
towards a certain text and began to prepare the sermon. Thoughts
just wouldn't come and I found great difficulty in finding enough to
say on the subject. I persevered but it seemed to me that anything
else I added was just padding and superfluous to the central theme. I
prayed about it but by the morning of the Sunday I was concerned
that I would look a fool with only ten minutes of worthwhile matter
to speak about, which, in those days fell well short of the 25minutes
usually expected. "It's no good, Dad," I said to my father. "I've only
got 10 minutes. I feel so inadequate. Perhaps I'm not cut out for this
after all." "Don't worry son," Dad said, "You just give your ten
minutes talk and then end. I'm sure they will understand."

As I cycled the seven miles from my home to Godshill, I was
praying, "Please, God give me something to say." I arrived at the
church in plenty of time and went up into the pulpit to find my
hymns and readings. One or two of the congregation turned up. Then
I was surprised to see George Tanner the blacksmith from Breamore
come in, as he was a preacher. He came up to me and asked me what
I was doing there as he had also received a request to preach there
that Sunday. Mr. Castle came at that point, apologised for the
confusion and we were just about to sort the service out when the
door opened and in came Mr Harry Pressey, a preacher in his late
nineties who was still very active. He too thought that he had been
asked to preach there that Sunday. By this time Mr. Castle, a frail and
gentle man, I recall, felt very embarrassed but we put him at ease and
said it didn't matter. Mr. Pressey said, "I'm old, so I would like to sit
down with the congregation." Mr. Tanner turned to me and said,
"We can do the service together. I'll tell you what, I'll give out one
hymn and you give out the next , I'll do one reading and you do the
next and when it comes to the sermon, I'll give ten minutes and **you
do ten minutes.**" My ten minute sermon was exactly right for the
occasion. My prayer had been answered in a very unexpected way.
Of course many would say that it was all a coincidence, and I must
confess there have been times when I have wondered about it, but at

the time I took it as a confirmation of a calling to be a lay preacher. Subsequently, after I had married and moved to another village, I became an accredited Local Preacher in the Methodist Church.

This story has a sequel, for some years afterwards I heard that the gentle Mr. Castle was possibly the late Barbara Castle's father-in-law. In 1995 I wrote to Baroness Castle and told her the story and asked if she could confirm the rumour. She wrote me a warm letter expressing her interest in the story and confirming that he lived in Godshill, and then went on to say: "Dad Castle was certainly one of the gentlest and most kindly people I have ever met. Devout without being priggish." She went on to say that she had frequent nightmares when due to address a meeting of thousands in the Albert Hall and had not got a word to say, but got through. "I suspect that when you were on your feet with your ten minute sermon you would have found inspiration to carry on for much longer than that."

Preaching Experiences.

Some have unkindly suggested that preaching satisfies one's ego and if it wern't for the buzz of being in the central position for an hour, many pulpits would be empty. I would dismiss this; for though some services are memorable and exciting, there are easier ways for one to gain an ego trip than sometimes struggling to interest a few people in a poorly attended cold chapel. Yet each week an army of unpaid lay preachers throughout our land spend hours studying and constructing their service, searching for ideas and illustrations so that the worshippers might capture something of what they believe to be the most important truth in the world.

To begin with, in the Methodist church as in most churches, there is a long period of training with exams and assessments. The preacher is subjected to questioning on his faith and there are trial sermons to be preached with ministers and experienced preachers in the congregation to report on his/her efforts. The fainthearted would soon fall by the wayside!

It took me over three years to become fully accredited. Each week the group would meet in Salisbury under a wonderful tutor, the Revd. Alan P. Ainsworth. Together we would explore the Bible and John Wesley's sermons! It was exhausting but so rewarding, for the Bible, which I knew was the "Word of God", became a site for personal encounter as I recognised God speaking through prophets, priests, kings and ordinary people and gradually revealing himself until he broke into human history in Jesus and showed himself to be all-loving and all-saving.

Those early years were not always easy. I didn't have a car and often had to cycle many miles. For distant appointments, it was arranged that three preachers would travel in the car of another preacher and we would be dropped off one by one. Sometimes we would be left at a cross roads half a mile away from the chapel and many times I have waited on a dark freezing cold night on a windswept Salisbury Plain for the driver to return, hoping that he didn't get carried away in his sermon!

On one occasion the driver had an old Austin 7 family car with a canvas hood. I was with another preacher on the back seat which was intended for children. My chin was on my knees. On the way back we stopped as we ascended a particularly steep hill. The engine slowed and we shuddered to a halt. We had to get out and

push the car up the hill before we could continue our journey home.

There have been times when I have been guilty of being too casual in my attitude. Once, in the early days, I cycled eight miles to a chapel, only to find that the service had started. I waited in the porch for the prayer to finish and entered, profusely apologising because I had not realised that the service started at 10.45am not 11.00am. However, the steward felt that I should be admonished in front of the whole congregation and proceeded to lecture me. "Time's time, my lad" he said. Almost in tears I entered the pulpit not knowing how to continue but the kind lady playing the organ bent over, so that the congregation couldn't see her, and whispered,

"Take no notice – just carry on as usual". They were to me sublime words of comfort and I did just that.

When a service has been received particularly well you feel both satisfied and guilty for perhaps your message was not meant to please but to stir. However, I ask forgiveness for being really pleased on one occasion because at the end I was showered with appreciation. As we left, the steward asked the driver if we would drop off an elderly member of the congregation as we passed his home. Of course the driver agreed and as the old man got out he thanked the driver for the ride and then turned to me and said. "Thanks lad, you will do all right - *presently*." Forty odd years have passed since then and I am still waiting for "presently" to come.

So I would humbly suggest that, with few exceptions, Lay Preachers are motivated by a belief that they have been called to proclaim the Gospel which they endeavour to do as best they can. They may not see great and dramatic response to their preaching but, having prayed and prepared diligently, they can then only leave it in the hands of Almighty God.

Easter Garden

Visit to the Holy Land

On our holiday in Israel, of course, we visited most of the famous holy sites. Amongst these was The Wailing Wall, (Western Wall) incorporating a part of Herod's Temple so important to the Jews, the Church of the Nativity at Bethlehem and the river Jordan where Jesus was baptised. Most enhanced our appreciation of the stories related in the Bible but to me the biggest disappointment was the Church of the Holy Sepulchre. The crowds might have put me off but the supposed tomb seemed contrary to my imagination of what it was like and the place of the Crucifixion didn't even give the impression of being on a hill, as recorded in the Gospels. Despite its sixteen hundred years of tradition I came away sceptical and confused.

I am so glad that our guide took us to the Garden Tomb sometimes called Gordon's Tomb because a General Gordon unearthed it. There are some who claim that it was the actual tomb in which Jesus was laid, being just outside the city wall and next to a cliff- like prominence with markings like a skull. Whether it was the actual site of the resurrection no one can know. To me it didn't matter. As I sat on a piece of rock surveying the scene and pondering over the Easter Story, I thought how right the setting was. The garden was radiant with flowers and trees as the evening sun cast an orange glow on the empty tomb. I was reminded of how a garden is transformed at springtime. For five months it has been held in the cold clutches of winter, when so much dies back and the outlook is drab, dreary and hopeless. Soon the warm sunny days of spring encourage the shoots to push their way through the softening soil, the buds begin to burst and by Easter the garden is ablaze with glorious colour. From death it has become alive again. I am reminded once more of the first Good Friday. Could there be a more desolate scene? Jesus, the one who had done so much good, who had given his followers cause for such hope, was dead.

No wonder the crowd went home "beating their breasts" and the disciples were in hiding. Winter had crept into their soul. Then the writer of St. John's Gospel continues the story with a detail of sheer genius (or was it inspiration?): 'Now, in the place where he was crucified, there was a garden'. It was here that Jesus rose from the dead and brought hope to the world. The garden now will have even more reason to be a symbol of life, joy and hope. From the base of the cross there blossoms a garden full of beautiful flowers like love, forgiveness and hope as expressed in this cherished verse: God loved the world so much that he gave his only son, that anyone who has faith in him will not die, but have eternal life.*

Mr. Clark's Devotion

Business had been poor and it seemed that every person who entered the shop was just enquiring, passing the time of day or worst of all complaining. The weather was atrocious and the staff for once were miserable. A cold wet February can be very depressing.

It was soon after lunch that Mr. Clark came in - an elderly, refined and kindly man. When I had finished serving him I enquired after his wife whom I knew had Alzheimer's disease and had been quite a trial to him, though he wouldn't have said so.

I felt I had some empathy with him because my father-in-law, who also suffered from this dreadful disease, had lived with us for five years and I knew the strain of living in a topsy turvy world where conversation at times was often irrational and sometimes bizarre.

"She's had a bad turn," he said, "and is now in hospital for a week or so. They say it will give me a break." He knew he could talk to me and related some of the recent disasters: how she refused to be dressed, how she disowned him and told him he is not her husband, how she threw her dinner over him and how sometimes he regretted having raised his voice to her. The list went on and I listened quietly. "I went in and sat with her this morning, just as I have every day this week. I stayed from 10 to 12 -30," he said. "Then they brought the lunch so I fed her just as I do at home. I kissed her good-bye and said that I would be back after I had eaten something myself. I returned shortly after two and she looked displeased. "Oh there you are, where have you been? You leave me here for days on end. I haven't seen you for a week. You don't care about me." He told me how he put his arms around her and tried to assure her of his love. "No, my dear, I haven't forgotten you. I come as often as I can. Of course I love you." He knew it was no good explaining that he had only been there two hours before. "I'm looking forward to you coming home again then I can take you out for a ride in the car. You like that, don't you? We will go out into the New Forest and across Cranborne Chase." His eyes lit up as he recalled some of the drives they had made in the locality when his wife was relaxed and interested. "Honestly, I can't wait for her to come home." His voice faltered and his face trembled. "You see, I love her. She can't help her illness. I know she doesn't really mean the things she says. After fifty years I'm only half a person without her and I want her home. I want to make her remaining years as happy as I can." By this time emotion was overtaking him and he departed in a hurry as I clumsily tried to tell him that I understood what he was saying.

Whenever someone suffers yet continues to love, I believe, the tragedy is transformed. One thing I am certain of – a man, whose "crucifixion" could not destroy his love, changed my working place on that drab wintry and depressing afternoon.*

Jilted but loved

Aunty Lillian was lovely. In my childhood eyes she was happy, kind and pretty. She was my Sunday school teacher when I first attended at the age of four and I still remember how the Bible stories she told became alive and real.

When I got older I asked my Mother, "Why didn't Aunty Lillian get married?" I couldn't understand why such a pretty girl should be single. Mum told me the sad story of how she had become engaged to her childhood sweetheart, a lovely lad called Winston, and how every one knew that they would eventually be married. The familiar sight of the couple walking happily hand in hand round the hamlet sparked in everyone joyful feelings as they anticipated the marriage which would surely come soon. Everyone thought that they were a most suitable couple. Then the bombshell! Winston suddenly broke off the engagement and it wasn't long before he left home and married another. I cannot judge him. He may have known of some incompatibility and his marriage did turn out to be a happy one; but the effect on Lillian was devastating. She cried and cried. My sister remembers her being brought to our house by her mother where she was left all day with my grandmother, a kindly Christian lady often used by the neighbours as a person who would listen and befriend those in trouble. Equivalent to the modern "Agony Aunt" or counsellor, I suppose.

Yet 60 years on I can't think of this break-up as a disaster. She had no children of her own but in a sense all the children in the hamlet became hers. All of us called her Aunty. She nursed her ageing mother till her death and it was Lillian whom people now called for when they were in need. She stayed with terminally ill people and befriended everyone. It would seem that despite her agony she was determined not to be embittered, but with God's help to do something useful with her life. My spirit is always lifted when I think of Lillian. In the place where she was "crucified" there was a garden which blossomed into beautiful flowers of love and kindness.

There is a moving hymn written by George Matheson the blind poet when he was jilted by his fiancée. It begins:

Oh love that wilt not let me go,
I rest my weary soul in thee:

The last verse is:

Oh cross that liftest up my head,
I dare not ask to fly from thee:
I lay in dust life's glory dead,
And from the ground there blossoms red
Life that will endless be.*

Blessed are the Merciful

The occasion was the Golden Wedding of a great aunt and uncle of mine. A special reception was held in the Village Hall and everyone was there. Well, not quite everyone. There was Roger, their youngest but surely he wouldn't come, would he? You see, at a time when marriage was deemed generally to be a lifelong commitment, he had left his own wife and fallen again for his boyhood sweetheart who meanwhile had married another, and taken her off to a distant town. When the husband arrived home from work he found a note on the table to say that his wife and three children had gone and wouldn't be coming back. Parents often try to give some excuse for their children's behaviour but Roger's Mum and Dad were as shocked as the whole village, which buzzed with gossip for weeks. They were ashamed of him and condemned his action though, of course, they still loved him.

Roger did write to his parents but he didn't call to see them for some while, and then it was only a fleeting visit because he sensed the hostility of the neighbours.

Now, some fifteen years on, the children had grown up and people's anger had abated, but even so few thought that Roger would attend his parents' special day. They were halfway through the reception when suddenly a silence descended on the happy gathering. Standing in the open doorway was Roger! I was told that you could cut the atmosphere with the proverbial knife. Obviously the loathing and anger were still there. He just stood, unable to move, frozen by the sudden change of mood. It was probably only for seconds but it seemed ages to those present. Then a cousin, who happened to be my father, and one of those gentle souls with a simple faith, got up from his seat and walked resolutely to the door. With his hand outstretched he said in a kindly voice, which because of the silence could be heard throughout the hall, "Welcome home, Roger. You've made your Mum and Dad's day." The ice was broken. With a few large steps Roger bounded to the top table and embraced his parents who were overjoyed. I was told that most of those present were fighting to keep back their tears.

Someone told me about it and I spoke to my father a few days later and asked how he came to be the one who made the first move. "I don't know," he said. "Whatever he'd done, I couldn't let him stand there frozen out. He'd come home and I just had to welcome him."

Winter had come to that happy Golden Wedding reception. The hostility, which had lain dormant until now, was suddenly unleashed. Then one man's forgiving spirit brought about a sudden Spring, which almost instantly transformed the place to a garden of joy.*

Alexander Cruden

How many people have heard of Alexander Cruden? Not many, I guess, yet amongst a certain group of people he is famous and his work is absolutely vital for them to perform their task with ease. He compiled a reference book known as Cruden's Complete Concordance to the Old and New Testaments. In it is almost every word that is in the Bible, listed alphabetically, with upwards of two hundred and twenty five thousand references, giving the chapter and verse in which the word is found. I have literally saved hours of time by referring to this book.

"What's remarkable about that?" you say. "All he had to do was to type or scan the text into a computer. The suitable software would sort it all out for him. A schoolchild could do it. The only limitation would be the speed and accuracy of the typing."

But listen; Alexander Cruden began his mammoth task in 1732. Using a quill for a pen he painstakingly wrote down every word and reference. Yet this great contribution to learning was not the ambition of the young Cruden. He had set his heart from an early age on being a Presbyterian minister. He attended the Grammar School at Aberdeen and later the Marischal College and was all set at the age of twenty one for his calling to be a minister of God. A living was found for him but, before he could take up his duties, he was stricken with a mental illness which was to dog him intermittently for the rest of his life. Bitterly disappointed, he knew it was impossible for him to achieve his ambition. After a few years as a private tutor, he came to London and opened a bookshop in the Royal Exchange. It was here that he conceived the idea and began to write his Concordance between bouts of depression. Can you imagine a more daunting or tedious task? Just think of the amount of page turning, as each word had to be written under the heading of its first letter. Despite his illness, his efforts were rewarded for the first edition was published in 1737. Both Oxford and Cambridge Universities were eventually to honour him for his work

Today, it is possible to obtain a Computer programme which

surely has made Cruden's Concordance redundant. I have tried it and discovered that, by the time the computer has warmed up and loaded, I have long found what I wanted in Cruden's celebrated work.

Alexander Cruden was "crucified" by a persistent illness that deprived him of his heart's desire, but his prayerful determination and dogged resolution despite all difficulties blossomed into a glorious garden of enlightenment, which has been of untold benefit to generations since.*

Thoughts from New Zealand

SHEEP

When you tell people that you are going to New Zealand it's not long before someone says: "Let me see, that's the place where there are more sheep than people, isn't it?" In fact there are far more sheep than people - some 60 million in comparison with 3.3 million humans.

From the time when some enterprising farmers introduced sheep in the l850s the economy of New Zealand has been dependent on them.

We saw sheep everywhere. On land, which looked so parched that it could not possibly contain any nourishment, to wide rolling plains with lush green grass rippling in the wind.

We were travelling in a camper van down a green sloping valley with a turn at the bottom, when suddenly we were confronted with a flock of sheep thickly sprawled out over the road in front of us. We may have hurled straight into them, but, just prior to seeing the sheep, I happened to see the flashing lights on the tractor driven by the shepherd and was ready to brake in time.

We watched as they were nudged by the two dogs into a gateway and we acknowledged this modern shepherd in jeans and check shirt as he waved a gesture of thanks to us for waiting. As we made our way I couldn't help thinking of the words in the 23rd Psalm: "Yea though I walk through the valley of the shadow of death I will fear no evil for thou art with me". I smiled to myself as I continued in my mind: "thy tractor and flashing light will comfort me." Certainly this would have been a valley of death but for the warning I had received from a very good shepherd who cared for his sheep.

I have noticed that the pages in the hymn books at a crematorium, which bears the hymn "The Lord is my Shepherd" is invariably tatty and smudged with fingerprints, such is its popularity. What is it about this Psalm which endears it to so many? I think it is because the similitude strikes a chord in the hearts of people. We identify ourselves in our extreme moments as being like sheep in need of a shepherd.

A lovely book by the late Leslie D. Weatherhead entitled "A Shepherd Remembers" crossed my mind as I watched those two dogs carefully ushering the sheep through the gate. He suggested that when the Psalmist wrote, "Goodness and mercy shall follow me all the days of my life", he was actually thinking of his sheep dogs, one called Goodness and the other called Mercy. It seemed to make sense to me as I saw the dogs bringing up the rear, coaxing the stragglers who had been distracted from following the shepherd.

In human terms the analogy is so fitting for "All we like sheep have gone astray." But, so often nudged by the sheer goodness and the tender mercy of God we find reflected in the most unexpected places, we are drawn once again to the Good Shepherd. Often we are not only brought back into line but feel we are part of a great gathering being led on a holy pilgrimage to that state of security, peace and happiness which has no end. That's why the Shepherd Psalm is so well loved. Essentially it's a song of comfort and hope.

"The Maddening Maze of Things. "

Wanaka is a charming town lying on the side of a beautiful lake bearing its name. "I do not know lake scenery that can be finer than this," enthused Trollope in 1842. We camped next to the lake which at dawn was as still as glass, reflecting the mountains now illuminated by the first beams of gentle light as the sun lifted over the opposite horizon. We were entranced by its beauty.

Just a mile up the road was a structure which was as ugly as the mountain scenery was beautiful, yet this too had something to say to me. Wanaka boasts that it has the first 3D maze in the world. It takes a minimum of 30 minutes to find your way to the four towers and back to the exit. The whole fenced-off area has over a mile of walkways and is complicated with bridges and stairways leading to each quadrant and many dead ends. We took a shade over ninety minutes to complete this walking puzzle. If we had run out of time there were emergency doors to allow us to escape.

I couldn't help thinking that life is a bit like a maze at times and usually by our own making. Often we upset God's plan for us and do our own thing, using the freewill he has given us, and life becomes traumatic. Sometime it seems that we have reached a dead end. I believe that it is then that God steps in and opens a new door so that we can set off in a new direction and find our way again.

There are times in life when we reach a crossroads like suffering, or bereavement or the corner of death itself, which we may approach with dread. We wonder just what is going to happen. Many people have found that God is there wanting to see them safely through.

At this very moment you may be a listener who can't sleep because you're worried over something. I can almost hear you saying, "Well, it's all right for you on holiday in New Zealand. You have no idea of my problems." That comment is fair for I'm sure that I have not suffered as much as many people. Even so I do know what it is like to be unable to sleep because of a problem which seems absolutely impossible to solve, and I have tossed and turned for hours on end. I have no glib answers but am assured that there always is a way out so don't give up looking for one.

Bearing in mind the things I have already said, may I humbly suggest that you try to be receptive to the notion that you are not alone: God is with you and he wants the best for you. You may find it difficult to talk to someone who up to now perhaps you didn't believe existed. But give it a try. After all, in the state you are now you've got nothing to lose. I pray that you will begin to see yourself - facing and working through the problem.

It was John Greenleaf Whittier who wrote:

> *Yet in the maddening maze of things,*
> *And tossed by storm and flood,*
> *To one fixed stake my spirit clings;*
> *I know that God is good!*

Contemplation

One of the things you must do if you visit the Mt. Cook region is to see the Fox Glacier. We walked the rather hazardous undulating path up to the terminal of the glacier. As we made our way, a teenage girl with a ponytail, tee shirt, jeans cut down to shorts and a backpack came up behind us. "Please, would you mind if I passed," she said. "Of course not," I replied, moving to one side to let her go by. "Thank you," she said as she bounded past. We watched as this slightly-built figure strode off with all the vigour and vitality of youth. "Oh to be young again," I said to my wife as we struggled up the slope.

We reached the face of the glacier. It was so big towering up above us with deep fissures and caves and constantly dripping water. As we approached, I noticed the girl on her own standing by the rope. "Would you like me to photograph you by the glacier?" I said. As soon as I started the sentence I wished I hadn't. Supposing she gives me the brush-off. "What a lovely idea," she said beaming all over her face as she handed me her camera. I took the photo and she appeared to be pleased. We walked further across the face of the glacier, filming continuously until we reached the torrent, which was evidence that the glacier is constantly melting.

One last shot of the great chasm from which the stream was emerging and we felt we had seen it all. We began to retrace our steps back across the bed of stones, scree and boulders which had been the base of the receding glacier. It was then that I noticed that this same girl had clambered up on to a huge boulder and was looking intently at the glacier. She didn't move, such was her concentration. "What a lovely shot," I thought to myself as I took my video camera out and prepared to capture this magic moment for posterity. She was still motionless. I did so want to record her profile as she contemplated the scene before her, but somehow I couldn't. I felt that I would be intruding into something deeply personal. Instead I began to look at what it was that so captivated her.

The sun was shining through a crevasse in the ice and looking from this position I could see the sparkling drops of crystal clear water dripping onto the ice below, sending up smaller jewels of water. The melting ice had taken on a gently shade of turquoise and in places there were curtains of transparent ice, beautifully perforated in a delicate filigree-like pattern. There was a movement and the girl clambered down but I was still looking at this miracle of natural beauty.

Almost directly, we moved off and I was still revelling in the wonder of it all as we walked up the steep narrow path. "Do you mind if I pass," a voice said. "Oh, it's you again," I said with a laugh as she ran briskly by and soon disappeared over the brow.

All I could do was to thank God that an unknown girl, who had time to stop and stare and take in the beauty before her had made me do the same.

Hell's Inferno ?????

One of the areas in New Zealand that I was very keen to visit was the Volcanic Plateau of Rotorua. The sulphuric fumes soon warn you that you are in the vicinity and it's not long before you see plumes of steam rising from field or forest. The geyser shooting boiling water 30 ft into the air is impressive and we were amazed at the site of the silica terraces. This is caused by a thin wide layer of thermal water, rich in chemicals, trickling down a gentle slope and leaving beautifully patterned deposits of various colours.

On our final day in the area we woke up to our first morning of rain so we visited Hell's Gate as we thought it would not interfere as much with the view. As it was, the rain made the bubbling mud pools and boiling lakes look even more forbidding because of the extra steam it caused. By the side of the pathways there were mud volcanoes. As the plopping mud shoots out it hardens, causing a rock mound increasing in size. Many of the active areas have sinister names like Sodom and Gomorrah, Devil's Cauldron and one, The Inferno, is a fierce, seething boiling pool of grey coloured-liquid. It is the hottest of them all as the graphite particles in the liquid allows the gurgling mass to rise 15 degrees above the boiling point of water.

It's no wonder that George Bernard Shaw who made a visit here in 1934 said, "Hell's Gate, I think it's the most damnable place I've ever visited and I would willingly have paid ten pounds not to have seen it. It reminds me too vividly of the fate theologians have promised me."

When I was young I have trembled under the preaching of some Hell Fire sermons, so I know just how frightening the highly figurative language of the Bible can be and I am glad that this kind of preaching is not generally practiced now. The problem is that the writers were trying to convey a spiritual truth by using words relating to a physical situation probably inspired by the burning rubbish heap outside the walls of Jerusalem. Many would say that Hell is now a taboo subject and not in tune with modern Christian

111

thought. However, considering it is mentioned 22 times in the New Testament I think that one should feel free to address it.

What then is Hell? No one really knows but it's all tied up with the notion that if a person continually rejects God, and all he stands for, then ultimately he will bring upon himself a separation from a grieving God who loves him. Imagine a player in an orchestra whose ear is so tone sensitive that if one instrument is slightly out of tune, he hears it immediately. He has a disagreement and leaves the orchestra in such a state that he loses his way down the corridor and finds himself in another hall where there is absolute bedlam. Here there are many budding musicians practicing in small groups and their various instruments are out of tune with each other. He has separated himself from all that he knew of harmony and this is Hell for him. Of course, I have fallen into the same trap as the Bible writers. I've tried to explain a spiritual truth with a physical human story and I know it is inadequate but it may just convey something of the truth.

Deep down we know where we belong. With the source of all that is Good, Beautiful, True and Loving and to know we have rejected this is a Hell some would say worse than the description from the Bible. Even so it is not the foreboding of such an eventuality which frightens us into response. Invariably, it is the loving nature of the person of Jesus which attracts us to Him.

G.A.Studgart Kennedy, the First World War padre and poet affectionately known as Woodbine Willie, wrote some powerful wartime poems. One I remember relates how a serviceman was telling his buddies about Christ and one verse went like this:

There ain't no throne, and there ain't no books
It's 'Im you've got to see.
It's 'Im, just 'Im that is the judge
Of blokes like you and me.
And, boys, I'd rather be frizzled up
In the flames of a burning 'ell
Than stand and look into 'Is face
And 'ear 'is voice say "Well?"

The Gold Rush

The desire to 'get rich quick' is not a new phenomenon. I suppose the State Lottery with its obscene jackpot of sometimes more than twenty million pounds must be the ultimate enticement. It is no surprise to me that many people whose lives are drab and with little hope of improving their position should be attracted, for it is offering what perhaps they think is their only hope. However, to the majority of people will it bring happiness?

These thoughts were in my mind as we drove through the Gold Field area of Central Otago on the Southern Island of New Zealand. Suddenly we saw some derelict workings on the hillside. There were rusty old sheds and some pits and caves. We stopped and entered the Kawarau Gorge Mining Centre. It was a brilliant hot day and there was no shelter from the sun but we decided it mustn't be missed so we walked round the entire site. This was only one of many sites in the Central Otago area. The first major Gold find was in 1861 and Gold Fever flared like a bush fire and spread outwards. In just four months four thousand men were swarming over the region, and a year later the population of just one field, the Tuapeka, was eleven thousand five hundred. If gold was plentiful, food was scarce for several miners starved to death. There just wasn't enough to go round and some speculators who arrived with food could become richer than some prospectors.

We were able to discover something of how hard the miners' lives were for a few huts had been re-erected just as they had been at the time. They were very small and extremely rough inside. Our tour ended with me trying my hand at panning some virgin soil from those very hills. You could just see a minute speck of this most sought after metal in the bottom of my pan but I lost it trying to pick it out! Not like the lady visitor who went to a special Gold Panning display being held in Queen Street, Auckland in 1971. The organiser had brought drums of "wash" from the old mines so those visitors could try their hand at panning. This lady was fortunate enough to pan a small nugget. It wasn't until afterwards it was learnt that she had taken it to a trading bank to have it valued. The bank wanted to know where she had found it. She told them she had panned for it in Queen Street. It seems incredulous but the bank advised her to obtain a "miner's right", as panning for gold was illegal without such an authority!

I suppose we all like the thought of getting 'rich quick', but it does have its dangers. A headline in a national newspaper said recently: "Once we sought Salvation in Religion, now 10 million prayers are raised for the National Lottery Jackpot."

There are more important things than money. You know it's true. Which is more important, your health and strength or a good bank balance; the happy smiling face of your child, arms up waiting to be lifted, or a Rolls Royce in the garage; for your spouse to say "I love you", or the gold ring on her finger which symbolises it?

Jesus said, "Lay not up for yourselves treasures upon earth …. but lay up for yourselves treasures in heaven."

Give Way

One thing the motorist from Europe will appreciate when travelling in New Zealand is the fact that there are so few cars on the road. You can travel for miles without seeing another vehicle. We found that the roads, even in isolated areas, were well maintained. The authorities had obviously saved money on the bridges, which were, almost inevitably, single track and you might also have to share it with a train! I was motoring along when suddenly I noticed the enormous word GIVE on the road. Around the corner the next word to be revealed is WAY and so the sentence builds up until I know what it is saying: GIVE WAY, ONE WAY BRIDGE.

I saw these words so many times that they became locked in my mind and I begin to repeat them just as, to the annoyance of others, you continuously hum a tune you've got "on the brain". Give way! Give way! I begin to think of times when one has to give way, or stick one's toes in and say, "I'm not going to move on this one."

A businessman is asked to do something borderline which, he realises, might help his client to avoid tax. It could lose him a lucrative sale and subsequent business to refuse but to Give Way is to begin the downward road to more serious forms of deception. Dilemmas like this require instant response and to do what one knows to be right demands a strong moral fibre.

Or perhaps, on a less serious level, do you Give Way and work on Sundays when, because Sunday is special to you, it hurts you to the core to do it. You feel enforced to join the Sunday rota by the attitude of your firm, and the fact that you have a family to support and a mortgage to pay, but you don't want to. To know whether to Give Way or stand firm often demands great strength of character and many pray for guidance.

Yet in some circumstances it is difficult but right to Give Way. In families there are often upsets and sometimes trivial things can blow up out of all proportion. I knew a family once where a dear lady and her husband lived happily with her brother for many years and then one day the two men fell out and vowed never to speak to each other again. What it was that caused the row I never knew but I do recall visiting that house on one occasion and doing business with them. The husband would turn to his wife and say, "You tell him that if he pays half I'll pay the other half." She turned to her brother and said, "Jack says if you pay half he'll pay the other half." "OK", said the brother, "You tell him that I'll pay my half if he pays his half". So this lady in a tense atmosphere was the intermediary because they had sworn never to talk to each other again. When I tell you that eventually one of them took his own life in a grisly fashion, I don't think you will be surprised. If only one of them had been willing to Give Way.

So much of the teaching of Jesus was interwoven with the thread of peacemaking, restoring relationships and forgiving people that he would have agonised on such a breakdown in a family.

If you grieve over an upset, whether the breakdown in relations is in the family, at work, or even in the church, don't be too proud to be the first to Give Way. Say, "Sorry if I've done something to offend. Let's put the past behind us, forgive and try to forget and be friends again." It's unlikely that you will receive a 'brush off' and the 'making up' will be so rewarding.

Powerful Symbols

On our first morning in New Zealand we took a bus to the beautiful city centre of Christchurch. The cathedral looks as English as any shire church back home and we are soon exploring its interior, starting with a climb up its tower to see the view of the old and modern Christchurch blended together.

Back in the chancel we admire the striking colourful embroidered altar cloth which, observed from a distance, depicts a pattern suggesting a fish, one of the oldest Christian symbols.

On the wall was a mural presented by the Cathedral Guild in 1885. It had so often provoked public comments that the authorities decided to place an explanation of its content. The problem was that its design included borders made up of the most despised symbol in the world, the swastika. Obviously the date shows that the designer intended no connection with Nazi Germany. The explanation goes on to say that the symbol is a Fylfot and is often found in ancient Christian art and I quote, "has found in theological thought the sanctity of its use". So Hitler had hijacked a religious symbol and changed the message to one of abhorrence, fear and violence. As memories fade, perhaps in years to come the message of the Fylfot will, in the minds of its beholders, once again revert to those of its glorious past in religious art.

There is one symbol that has changed its meaning for all time. I am referring to the simple form we know as "The Cross". A symbol which was more dreadful in its connotation than the scaffold, for here men were subjected to a slow tortuous death known as crucifixion, Yet that same symbol today is a sign of hope, peace, love and joy. The reason for this is that Christians believe that God himself loved the human race so much that he came to this earth to save it. His righteousness, His compassion for people in need, His condemnation of evil made Him enemies and the inevitable happened and He was put to death on a cross. But on the first Easter Sunday He rose from the dead and imparted a message of hope to his friends who saw Him. Later they were to be filled with Christ's

Spirit and became a powerful mobilised company that set the then known world ablaze with His good news of love, sacrifice and hope. The cross became the symbol of their witness and comes to us today bearing the same Good Tidings: That God did not despair of humanity but had given us all a chance to repent and accept His salvation. So that's how the meaning of the cross was transformed and has become such a powerful symbol for all that is good.

Before the demise of the USSR, I went to Moscow and was surprised to see this Christian symbol dominating the skyline of the Kremlin. There it was blazing away in sparkling gold, surmounting the onion dome pinnacles of buildings which were once churches.

I wondered if some of the devout Christians of those dark times used to look up at those crosses and be constantly reminded of God's love for them as shown in Jesus, and went on with their life confident that in the end all would be well.

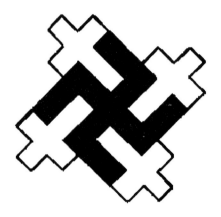

No Greater Love

Ron and Mary Harris emigrated to New Zealand some twenty years ago when their two boys were young. We knew that Andy, the younger of the two, was a mountain guide on New Zealand's highest mountain, the spectacular Mount Cook.

It was in May 1996 as we were watching the news on TV that we suddenly pricked up our ears. We thought they had said that three climbers from New Zealand had been killed on Mount Everest and one of those named was Andrew Harris. It was confirmed on later news bulletins so we decided to ring Ron but couldn't get through. In a few days Ron contacted us. Ironically, they were on holiday in the UK. Of course it was their Andy and their grief was intense. The only consolation, at that time, was that he had died doing what he most enjoyed. Ron said that after scaling Everest the weather had deteriorated and it seemed he had just walked out of the bivouac.

Later, we received from them a fuller account of the circumstances in which he died. Jon Krakauer, an American mountaineer and writer who was on the expedition, gave a report here abbreviated.

As they were descending, other climbers further down had heard over the radio the repeated cries for help from their friend Rob Hall in a bivouac near the south summit, saying that Doug Hansen had collapsed and that they both desperately needed oxygen. It was Andy who decided to go to their assistance. A descending Sherpa from the South Summit had met and talked to him as he struggled back up the summit ridge though the storm had set in and the weather was atrocious. The Sherpa recalls looking back and seeing Andy who, despite being utterly exhausted, was continuing to plod slowly back up the summit ridge alone to assist his friends. Andy would surely have known the dangers and that he ought to immediately descend. Instead, because of compassion, he chose to go back into the "death zone" of the mountain in one of its fiercest storms to help the two in distress. No- one heard of Andy after that, though in the morning of 11th. May 1996 Rob Hall did report in a distraught final radio message: "Andy was with me last night but he doesn't seem to be with me now. He was very weak." Andy's visit was confirmed because his ice axe was found next to Rob. For his outstanding bravery H.M. the Queen confirmed that Andrew should be awarded, posthumously, The New Zealand Star for Bravery.

Our memory of Andy was blurred because of distance and time so it was difficult to enter into the experience of the family's tragic loss. However, it came home to me when I read how a very proud Ron took a commemorative plaque to Queenstown and there in a Rose Garden, next to Captain Scott's memorial, he chiselled away himself at the rock and fixed a permanent reminder of his son's sacrifice.

It was Jesus, who was to come to know all about sacrifice, who said, "No greater love hath any one than to lay down his life for his friends."

Sermons Remembered

Drain Pipes or Organ Pipes

I recall a friend of mine who was a theological student telling me how every student in his college had in turn to preach a sermon to the whole assembly of students and lecturers. Afterwards the sermon was dissected by everyone, though it was intended to be constructive criticism. One Sunday a student valiantly delivered his sermon only to receive from one of the professors a scathing assessment of the content. "You have brought the pulpit into disrepute by one totally inappropriate illustration," he said. "It was unworthy of your high calling and I trust I shall never hear a student or anyone else use such a disgraceful allegory in a pulpit again."

What was the outrageous illustration which caused such an outburst and almost reduced the unfortunate student to tears?

Apparently he had been saying that in the sight of God everyone was equal and every task however small and humble was important to Him. "Whether you are a Bishop or a church cleaner, an actress or the scene mover, the Queen or the chambermaid, you are all of equal concern to Him. The important thing is everyone should endeavour to do his or her job well". Unfortunately for him, the student went on to emphasise his point by saying: "We are all like pipes. We could be organ pipes doing a very glamorous and showy job, or we could be drain pipes doing a very mean unpleasant job. Everyone takes for granted the humble drain pipes as they relentlessly continue day and night to quietly remove the waste from our cities, but the organ pipes are made to be noticed by everyone in hearing distance. Yet we all know that both are of great worth." He went on to say that society was held together by countless numbers of people quietly doing their perhaps humdrum job with few recognising their importance.

When this story was related to me I felt sorry for the student. To me the illustration, though perhaps he could have found a more tasteful example, was very apt, and, far from bringing the pulpit into disrepute, it conveyed to the congregation in a graphic way an essential truth.

We are not equal in ability. That is painfully obvious but we are all equal in our capacity to achieve the best we can.

Maybe the kind of job we do is highly skilled but by its very nature does not attract much attention. Perhaps our job for various reasons is simple, monotonous and not too demanding, or perhaps we are out of regular paid employment and spend our time doing many unspectacular things. At this very moment *(in the middle of the night)* there are many people doing important jobs, some humble and others incredibly skilful, but because they are done in the hours of darkness few appreciate them. Whatever task we do, to God we are all important because we all have a part to play in His world. It was George Herbert the hymn writer who wrote:

> Teach me my God and King,
> In all things thee to see.
> And what I do in anything,
> To do it as for thee.
>
> A servant with this clause,
> Makes drudgery divine.
> Who sweeps a room as for thy sake,
> Makes that and the action fine.

Hitting out For God

Isn't it strange how some things remain in your mind and others, for no apparent reason, are forgotten forever? I must have heard hundreds of sermons, lectures and addresses but I can only remember a handful.

One short address was by my friend Rev. John Dover some 45 years ago. He was still at school, a keen sportsman, and already a gifted orator. It was a Camp Weekend when all the young people of our group of churches spent two nights under canvas. It was a remarkable weekend for many reasons but John's short address is as vivid to me now as it was then. It came to my mind recently when I heard the news that the famous English cricketer, Dennis Compton, had died.

John was making the point that sometimes it is necessary for us to be courageous and take risks in our spiritual life and, after mentioning great people who had done just that, he referred to cricket and the Test Match which had just concluded. Those were the days of Dennis Compton, a quality batsman, renowned for attacking the bowling. "Not the sort of man to 'poke' around the crease with the bat," said John. "He was adventurous and hit out hard and strong. No wonder the ball was usually destined for the boundary. Of course he took risks but his style was attractive and the aim was to win." John then went on to say that we should be prepared to 'hit out' for our beliefs. If we are for ever cautious, afraid that we might make mistakes, our mission will be dull and uninspiring and playing safe doesn't always protect us from blunders anyway.

John was to become a very effective Christian minister. A renowned preacher who never minced his words even when on one occasion he had the entire Cabinet including the Prime Minister in his congregation. Sadly, John died in his forties but his witness continues in the books he wrote and the recurring memories of his friends. St. Peter the apostle was a man who 'hit out' for God. An impulsive character anyway, Jesus had to restrain him when his impetuosity got the better of him. It was Peter who argued when

Jesus said he would have to die. It was Peter who cut off the soldier's ear in Gethsemane and reaped Jesus' disapproval and later, when Jesus walked on the water it was Peter who jumped into the water to meet him. After Pentecost there was no holding Peter back. He took every opportunity to preach the gospel and he went on preaching boldly even when threatened and persecuted. "We cannot stop telling about the wonderful things we saw Jesus do and heard him say," he told his persecutors.

I confess I fall short in this department content often to "poke around at the crease" especially when there's controversy. God grant that all of us who have a faith at all will be prepared to 'hit out' for what we believe.

Thinking Aloud

Injustice Remembered

Why is it that at the most unlikely times something springs to your mind which causes your heart to beat faster, your muscles to tense and your complexion to change suddenly to a bright red? A friend of mine once told me how he woke up one morning, sat up in bed and clenched his fist in rage because it suddenly crossed his mind that a bus driver had turned his two children off the bus some two miles from home because they didn't have enough money for the whole journey. He recalled how he had gone out to see where they were because they were late, only to find his two frightened little girls walking hand in hand along this lonely country road. He was outraged by the incident and reported it in no uncertain terms and received an apology from the company. Yet here he was some thirty years after fuming over the injustice and risk of the episode. He began to smile to himself as he realised how silly it was to get hot and bothered about something that happened so many years ago. What ever was the point of it? What good does it do any one remembering it now? At first I agreed with him, but then it struck me that there is a difference between forgiving and forgetting. To forgive means that you don't hold it against the person who has wronged you but you don't forget the incident and often the memory of the occasion helps you to perpetuate the idea that nothing like this should be allowed to happen again.

When Martin Luther King Junior had become famous for his civil rights campaigning, he never forgot some of the injustices which had been inflicted on him. He would recall one of his early memories of how he used to play with some white children who lived nearby his home in Atlanta. When he was six he went to the Negro elementary school and his friends went to the white school. It was at this point that the parents of the white children decided to draw the colour line. Out of the blue they told him the harsh facts that he wasn't to call round and play with them any more because "we are white and you are coloured." He ran home crying to his mother who took him on her lap and, because he was intelligent, explained to him the story of his forefathers, of being taken from Africa and sold into slavery. How the whites, even after slavery was abolished, still thought that they were superior. She told him that this treatment of blacks was happening all the time and that he must realise it would happen to him too but she ended by saying, "You're just as good as anybody else".

Fortunately Martin Luther King never forgot that episode or the many other insults, abuses and physical violence meted out to him.

At his funeral the Eulogy was given by Benjamin E. Mays, President Emeritus at Moorhouse College. He said: *"If any man knew of the suffering King knew. House bombed; living day by day for thirteen years with the constant threats of death; maliciously accused of being a Communist; falsely accused of being insincere and seeking the limelight for his own glory; stabbed by a member of his own race; slugged in a hotel lobby; jailed over twenty times; occasionally deeply hurt because his friends betrayed him - and yet this man had no bitterness in his heart, no rancour in his soul, no revenge in his mind; and he went up and down the length of the world preaching non-violence and the redemptive power of love."*

The secret which enabled him not to harbour resentment was his closeness to God. After a press conference in which he poured out his soul to great effect, a pressman asked him, "What has happened to you since last night? Have you talked to anyone?" And Martin replied, "No. I haven't talked with anyone. I have only talked to God."

I'm so glad that Martin Luther King remembered the injustices which were meted out to him.

Twinning

I'm an unapologetic "Twinner" for this movement has given me untold pleasure. It was back in 1981 that my local town, Fordingbridge, after delving into the possibilities and making exploratory visits, first signed the documents which for all time linked our town with the vibrant town of Vimoutiers in Normandy. Of course there are civic ceremonies, processions and banquets but it's not for that reason I am a convinced "twinner". My enjoyment from twinning can be summed up in one word – Friendship.

Relationships between the French and the English have certainly been strained over the years and national patriotism still often rears its head. One has only to watch a soccer or rugby match between our countries to realise that this is one needle match which must be won!

To be honest, I am sometimes irritated by seemingly hostile comments made by French politicians and I guess that the French are equally upset by what our leaders say. But the amazing thing is that, in the many exchanges I have experienced with the people of Vimoutiers, I have only found warmth and friendship. Sometimes they have even apologised for some extreme comment by a leader in Paris! When they invite you into their home they take you into their hearts and their generosity and hospitality are quite over-whelming.

During the war their town was subjected to the usual pressures placed on a community by an invading army yet it remained largely intact. However, after D.Day as the Battle of Normandy drew to its bloody conclusion when the Falais Gap was closed, erroneous intelligence informed the allies that the Nazis were regrouping in Vimoutiers. The order went out that it should be bombed. Vimoustearins, though aware of the danger, were rejoicing that liberation was soon to be theirs. Then a warning came through that the inhabitants should gather in the Church of Notre Dame in the centre of the town. Most of them did and the church with its elegant twin spires was spared but the rest of the town was flattened. Some two hundred of the inhabitants were killed on that dreadful day by the liberators.

It would be understandable if the people were to become insular and desire to just get on with life in their own way but they wanted to be magnanimous and in 1969 twinned with the German town of Sontra: and in 1979 when we approached them we discovered that they were actively seeking a British twin. We were officially wedded in 1981/82. Since then we have experienced many happy occasions with our French friends and have made friends with the Germans from their Twin town.

I was asked to give the eulogy at the funeral of one of the architects of their Twinning, in whose home I had found such warmth and where I met some of our German friends for the first time. After paying tribute to her outstanding contribution to the Twinning cause, I felt compelled to end with the text from the Sermon on the Mount: "Blessed are the Peacemakers".

The Incidental Detail

I often think it's the incidental details that make all the difference to a story. From being a mere factual account the narrative becomes a captivating and visual picture. That's why some newspaper articles and radio talks are so gripping for the writer which, by including those seemingly superfluous extras, paint a scene which is memorable. The longest running series of talks, "Letter from America" by Alistair Cooke, I believe, owes its popularity not only to the friendly voice and graphic presentation of the main theme, but also to those short "by the way" side issues and observations which light up the account.

Likewise I think it is the incidental details which make many of the Bible narratives so vivid. You suddenly come across a detail which illuminates the whole scene and the story becomes alive.

After Jesus had been arrested and was taken away, St Mark tells us that the impetuous disciple, Peter, followed. It's here we find the incidental detail. St Mark adds colour to the story by saying that Peter followed *at a distance*. Immediately we can picture Peter furtively dodging from tree to tree, pillar to pillar, trying to keep up with the platoon of soldiers which was escorting Jesus to his judgement. Then when they arrive at the Priests' Courtyard, St Mark gives us some more seemingly erroneous information. He tells us that Peter stayed sitting among the attendants, *warming himself in front of the fire*. Come to think of it, this was a bold but not so clever move on Peter's part, to try and get "lost" amongst the crowd jostling to keep themselves warm. Perhaps it was the light of the fire that revealed him. The amazing thing is that this apparent trivial observation becomes the backcloth for the whole sad story of Peter's infamous denial. I find such details fascinating and to me they give the story a ring of truth. This is not so surprising if, as is generally thought, Mark was present during those last fateful days. There is also strong evidence that Mark was Peter's secretary, so he most probably heard the story countless times from Peter's own lips.

Another account, this time in the Gospel of St John, rings true because of its quite unnecessary yet graphic detail. They brought to Jesus a loose-living woman who had been caught in the very act of adultery. For this she could face an arbitrary death penalty by stoning whilst the man involved would get off scot-free. Jesus was teaching near the Temple when the Teachers of the Law and the Pharisees presented him with the lady and challenged Jesus with the law of Moses which says that she should be put to death. This was a trick question for they knew that he would not agree with such a barbaric injustice. The story continues that *Jesus bent over and wrote with his finger in the dust.* What value has this detail to the main thrust of the story other than being the memory of someone who couldn't forget it? Jesus straightened up and said "Whichever one of you has committed no sin let him be the one who throws the first stone" and then *he bent over again and continued writing on the ground.* Perhaps Jesus, by bending down, was giving the observers an opportunity to slip away without embarrassment There is no record as to what Jesus was writing. Perhaps the observer could not read, or perhaps he wasn't near enough, but the action was dramatic enough to be indelibly imprinted on his mind. I can only imagine the silence broken solely by the scuffle of feet as her accusers melted away. Jesus straightened up again and said, "Where are they? Is there no-one left to condemn you?" "No one, sir," she replied. "Then neither do I condemn you. Go on your way but don't sin again".

Humility

At a school assembly I related a modern version of the story Jesus told of the Pharisee who went to pray at the temple and said how good he was: "I fast two days a week and I give you a tenth of my income. I thank you, God, that I am not greedy, dishonest or an adulterer and not like that wretched tax collector over there." The man he was referring to had also gone to pray and all he could say was, "Please, God, forgive me, I know I have done evil things." "Which person do you like best?" I asked the assembly. Instantly they replied, "The tax collector." Why should a crowd of spirited, successful and exciting thirteen year olds identify with a self-demeaning and apparent ultimate loser so readily?

I am reminded of the story of the priest of the little continental town of Ars. He was a humble man and no doubt his fellow clerics in the diocese would have said that he had a lot to be humble about!

Knowing of his lack of learning, many sent him letters saying that he was a disgrace to the cloth and that they would all sign a petition asking the Bishop to have him removed. He replied to them all with gratitude, begging the prayers of his correspondents, "that I may do less harm and more good." The petition was sent round to the clergy to be signed in turn by each of them. One priest, either from bravado or remorse, sent it to the Priest of Ars (Curé D'Ars) himself who tearfully read what it said about him being incompetent and ignorant, and he remorsefully put his signature with the rest. When it arrived on the Bishop's desk there was embarrassment to see the priest's own signature boldly there with the others.

Some then felt that his inner quality of humility made up for many of his trivial failings.

Why is it that I like that story and find myself drawn to this little man who seems to have been a bit of a failure? I think it is because today when the world applauds excellence, perfection and self assurance in all things, qualities that some of us know we

are unlikely to attain, the story of someone who knew his imperfections and was sorry for them strikes a chord in all of us.

Is nothing Sacred?

It seems that all my heroes are being shot at. I read the other day that Horatio Nelson of Trafalgar fame was a malingerer who exaggerated his eye damage to try and get a pension. Of course, members of the Nelson Society dispute this but for me the damage was done.

Then I saw a TV programme which suggested that Lawrence of Arabia made up some of his experiences in his book "The Ten Pillars of Wisdom". My romantic dream of the Englishman with flowing Arabian dress riding a camel over the desert dunes "bit the desert dust".

Then, to crown the lot, a celebrity took a swipe at Mother Teresa saying that she was her pet villain. She seemed to be questioning her motives. Can you believe it?

To begin with, I'm shocked and outraged, not so much because of the possible failings of my heroes, but at the realisation that some people out there are prepared to devalue the fond memories of the great, possibly just to be sensational. The sadness is that when indiscretions are raked up years after someone's death when they are unable to defend themselves, it is these we tend to think of first rather than all the good the person has done.

To come to terms with these disclosures, I forced myself to remove my heroes from the pedestal where I had placed them and to see them as they really were. None of them pretended to be perfect. They were fallible human beings who did make mistakes, form poor judgements and go contrary to their own conscience just like the rest of us.

Ffyona Campbell walked nineteen thousand five hundred miles round the world. It was a tremendous feat of discipline and endurance which captivated the world. Then a year after, she came clean and admitted that for one thousand of those miles she was sitting in the back-up van. Secretly, she went back and walked those thousand miles, but even that didn't release her from her sense of guilt so she decided she had to confess to the world. I don't know how this story strikes you but whereas before I just admired her tenacity in walking round the world, now her confession endears me to her for ever, for that took real courage. The point is, as it says in St. Paul's letter to the Romans, every one has sinned and is far away from God's saving presence but have we the courage to admit it to ourselves, confess it to God, let alone tell our family and the world?

An Expert

"Please Lord, preserve us from experts," I heard someone say the other day. She was referring to one of the new ideas promoted by the so-called pundits which turns out eventually to be terribly flawed.

I'm rather sorry that all experts have been tainted by this accusation because I have been served well by them. Accountants, surveyors and lawyers have given me very sound advice and in some cases have saved me money and lots of worry. Even in mundane matters I have been glad of their information.

When our children were young we entertained a visitor. It was early summer and we went for a stroll round our garden. Suddenly he said "There's a blackbird's nest over there." "How do you know?" we asked. "Because I noticed its movements," he said. Sure enough, when we investigated we found the nest. Shortly after he continued, "Hush, for a moment, please." We stood perfectly still: "There's a wren's nest over there. I think I can hear the chicks." He was right again. Unknown to us he was also an amateur ornithologist. He found nine bird's nests in our garden hedge that afternoon, and though I'm a 'country lad' I was unaware of them. An expert had opened up a whole new interest in our garden. And the children were enthralled.

I once read a book called, "How to live to be one hundred." I must say that I read it with more enthusiasm when I noticed that its author wrote it when he was ninety-six years old! A definition of the word "expert" is someone with special knowledge so I reckoned that this author was an expert because he had learnt from experience.

Similarly I enjoyed conversations with and heeded the wisdom of Fred Jones, a character who lived in our locality. He had been a scoundrel, an alcoholic and the scourge of the village. He gave his parents a terrible time. Generally vulgar and uncouth he admitted that, when drunk, he often went to bed with his dirty boots on. One evening he reluctantly entered the village chapel at the invitation of a friend. The words he heard affected him deeply and he became a Christian. At The Cuckoo Inn his friends said, "Give him a week"

135

then "Give him a month. He'll be back." Incredibly, he never drank again. He became a gentle and respected resident and eventually a preacher himself, claiming that in the chapel that night Christ had come into his life.

I would sit spellbound listening to Fred Jones for, though he only received an elementary education, to me he was an expert in the field of religion because he was a living example of a man who by the grace of God was changed for the better.*

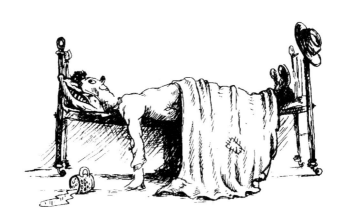

Icons

I was in Russia before the downfall of Communism and we were taken into the Assumption Cathedral in the Kremlin, then a museum. The colours of the frescoes and icons were spectacular and I wanted to film them but I had noticed a sign showing a camera with a cross through it. Suddenly it dawned on me that they were implying that by filming I was desecrating the place, whereas it was the Communists who had driven the priest out and forbidden the place to be used for its rightful purpose - to praise almighty God. I then did something of which I am not proud. I took the lens cap off my video camera and walked around surreptitiously filming the icons and paintings with the camera lying against my chest. It was not only wrong but a stupid thing to do, and I could have been arrested and my camera confiscated. Inevitably I was noticed and a lady commissar came up and ordered me to put the lens cap on and put the camera back in my case. I was frightened but couldn't help smiling when I noticed that all my friends had just melted into the crowd! They had disowned me. The official then proceeded to follow me around, which did rather spoil my visit. However I had in a short time taken a video of beautiful pictures of the icons that play such an essential part in the religious life of the Eastern Orthodox Church and they did stimulate my interest.

Though I do regret breaking the law of a country in which I was a guest, I do not feel what I did was wicked. Many are beautiful paintings of Christ, the Virgin or one of the saints and often contain symbolic objects which define the meaning. Their primary object is as a focus for prayer and devotion. On the same holiday we visited an Inuit home on the Tundra and there on the shelf was a small discoloured icon of Christ which was intended to focus one's thought when praying.

I have no problem with aids to worship but an icon, like many symbols, can become an idol and, far from leading individuals to worship God in spirit and truth, become to them a God with supposed magical powers. When we visited Nicaea in Turkey we were shown the ruins of St Sophia where the seventh Vatican Council was held in 787AD. Among other things this council declared that icons deserved "reverence" not "adoration". This was to lead to the final rift between Constantinople and Rome when the Eastern Orthodox Church and the Roman Catholic church went their own ways.

My rather old dictionary only defines an icon as an "image, statue, painting or mosaic of sacred personage" but another meaning for the word icon has come into common use. The media often talk about Pop Idols as "Icons of our age," Some would refer to the late Princess Diana in this way. I must say that the Princess would be top in my book if I wished to choose a symbol of someone who was compassionate and cared for people. Even so, the word icon in this sense is still tied to the celebrity being idolised by the masses, something which the Princess herself did not encourage. There is yet another modern meaning. Today many people are more familiar with the word "icon" as used in computer jargon. Essentially it is a representative small image which simplifies the access to a program. By this means it became easy for anyone to use the computer and so the popularity of the PC suddenly took off.

These three types of icons can, I believe, have a common meaning, for essentially an Icon is a *pointer* to something or some one else far more important than the mere image you see.

Next time you use your mouse and place the pointer on an icon to open a wonderful program, think of the little Russian Inuit woman looking at her discoloured icon of Christ and pray that, rather than believe that it has any mystical value in itself, it might remind her of the true glorious nature of God.

Perception

It's not only how things actually are but also how they are perceived that's important. Recently I closed my shop and retired but for years I have spent thousands of pounds trying to get across to the public that, if they examined my prices and services, my deals were often better than the large stores. Unfortunately so often they were unable to perceive that I could possibly compete with the "big boys" and just wouldn't bother to enquire.

I read recently how a coloured doctor on board an aircraft heard his name called and observed the stewardess walking down the gangway to his seat. When she saw that it was a black person sitting in the seat she began asking the white people in front and behind because she could not perceive that this man could possibly be a doctor. I think it is a tragedy that such perceptions still exist yet we know that prejudice is often almost an unconscious attitude. What can be done to rectify such blatant misconceptions? Some think the answer is education and have poured money in to change people's views.

Because the perception of the teaching profession had reached such an all time low affecting the recruitment of good quality teachers, a public relations company was appointed at a cost of two million pounds to extol the qualities of the teaching profession.

The answer, I suppose, is education but sometimes our actions can cause people to have misconceptions. Take the church for instance. We can't wonder that some people perceive it as being obsessed with money and buildings because, for some, their only contact is when there is an appeal for something like the roofing or organ funds. Actually, its aim and inspiration is to serve in the name of Jesus Christ whose whole mission prompted by love was to serve and save the world. The Salvation Army who, though it does regularly conduct nationwide door to door money-raising appeals, is generally perceived by the public to be a caring organisation because they see them serving the homeless, the lost and deprived.

On the other hand the mainline churches, though also doing some good caring work, possibly tend to be seen as money-grabbing businesses.

Recently I attended a seminar which extolled the virtues of Churches featuring on the Internet. My group was asked to design a Home page for a particular church. We featured a picture of the church building as a kind of logo. When this was produced for the combined groups, I wanted the ground to swallow me up for the leader nearly tore his hair out. "Buildings again," he shouted. "Why are we so obsessed with buildings? A page like that would send out the wrong message - something the church is so adept at doing. Why can't we feature some area of caring which the church is doing? After all, the real church is the people." Suitably admonished, I could see his point. Perception is so important yet maybe God, who sees us as we really are, also sees that predominantly our preoccupation is with things rather than with people. Maybe it's not the image that has to be changed but the core.*

Treaty of Versailles

On a recent visit to the palace of Versailles, as I walked through the famous Hall of Mirrors I was suddenly conscious of the significance of a happening here which occurred 80 years ago this week. In this very room was signed the ignominious Treaty of Versailles which many historians believe provided the fertile soil on which the fascists' seeds grew, resulting in the Second World War. A cold shiver flowed down my spine as I realised that maybe all the brutality, hatred, heartbreak and blood shed which enveloped Europe and beyond may have stemmed from discussions which took place in this magnificent room. As I looked out of the window and scanned the beautiful view of the formal gardens and lawns which like a carpet drifted away to a border of trees, in my mind's eye I could see a Europe ablaze with distorted bodies and agonised faces. There was row upon row of white tomb stones that flowed away to the horizon in an imaginary military cemetery.

What was the flaw in this Treaty which many think caused such a dreadful consummation? The fatal defect was that the treaty contained excessive demands from the German people as retribution for the war which had so harshly consumed people and places.

To a nation beaten and crushed by arms, the victorious allies imposed conditions which not only sought to cripple Germany militarily and territorially but also to punish them severely economically. Not only were many brought to the point of starvation by the impossible reparations demanded, but there was also rampant inflation. It is said that hungry folk would arrive at a bakers with a wheelbarrow full of marks to buy a loaf of bread. There was widespread unemployment and utter despair. Worst of all, the proud German people were totally humiliated.

Is there any wonder that, when a figure emerged who promised to deliver and lift them from wallowing in their inferiority, that they should embrace him with fanaticism? So Hitler and his Fascist henchmen made their disastrous entry into twentieth century history. Thankfully, a better way was pursued after the Second World

War but today we remember that extracting excessive retribution is not the best way to begin a future of peace.

St Paul writing to the Romans said: *Never pay back evil for evil. Let your aims be such as all men count honourable. If possible, so far as it lies with you, live at peace with all men. My dear friends, do not seek revenge, but leave a place for divine retribution; for there is a text which reads, 'Justice is mine, says the Lord, I will repay.' But there is another text: 'If your enemy is hungry, feed him; if he is thirsty, give him a drink; by doing this you will heap live coals on his head.' Do not let evil conquer you, but use good to defeat evil.* (NEB Rom. 12, 17-21)

Father God, as we remember the past, help us not to hold grudges or seek revenge but always to look for avenues towards reconciliation.

One Every Three and a Half Seconds

It was the Hungersite on the Internet which made an impact. The Home page depicts a map of the world and every 3.6 seconds a different country in the Third World becomes momentarily black to signify the death of another person from starvation. Then I read the text which said that it is estimated that one billion people in the world suffer from hunger and malnutrition. That's roughly 100 times as many as those who actually die from these causes each year.

About 24,000 people die every day from hunger or hunger-related causes. This is down from 35,000 ten years ago, and 41,000 twenty years ago. Three-quarters of the deaths are children under the age of five.

Famine and wars cause about 10 per cent of hunger deaths, although these tend to be the ones you hear about most often. The majority of hunger deaths are caused by chronic malnutrition. Families facing extreme poverty are simply unable to get enough food to eat.

As I looked at the map, I tried to imagine the heartache and desolation of a mother as she watches her poor emaciated child die. I find it very difficult to relate as I should to my image of an African lady outside her hut, crying over her lifeless baby. Over the years we have seen the painful pictures on our TV screens so often and we may even look away muttering to ourselves: "Not again!". Yet we are forced to look, and the pathetic sight of hungry whimpering children wrings from our hearts sympathy and yet at the same time anger and frustration. Anger, because our quiet evening has been disturbed and frustration from a feeling that we feel we can do nothing about it. In Central Africa alone at the moment fourteen million people are under threat, and as soon as this particular crisis is over somewhere else another will begin. I just can't get my mind round it. I know that I have got to try, not just to salve my conscience, but because those children are just as important as our own children and grandchildren, just as loved, just as precious. For a moment I am going to forget the masses who face starvation. I am going to think of just one child I know. My mind pictures a child whom I love, healthy, happy and full of fun. I can feel my face breaking into a smile immediately as I think of him. He's a lovely child and so precious.

Thinking about him I force into my mind's eye the image of a walking skeleton with a bloated tummy, shedding tears of hunger, and for a moment I'm there. Another 3.6 seconds have passed and another country goes black on the world map signifying the death perhaps of that little child in my mind who is just as important and loved as the one who is so precious to me.

I resolve that I am going to forget the twenty four million. The number is so massive I feel I can't do anything meaningful about it; but that one little child, to whom I have briefly related by coupling to a boy I know, is one for whom I ought to have done something. I pray that I will not be allowed to forget it.

If I had my Way

It's a good rule of thumb that if you want to make a point you choose the best time to do it effectively. Unfortunately, sometimes it seems there never is a good time. I want to say something which could sound offensive and heartless to some people at any given time but I assure you that it has been on my mind for years and I have been waiting for the right time to say it. I think you will soon understand my reluctance in expressing my concern because, inevitably, as soon as I open my mouth, tragically another event will occur and I will feel that people might think I am being incredibly insensitive and thoughtless. But I have decided that if I don't say it now, it might never be said.

My concern is about what happens after a sudden national disaster, whether natural or man-made.

There is not one of us who hasn't been moved and distressed by the shocking, heart-rending scenes on our television as we have intruded into the grief and despair of devastated survivors and relatives of those who have perished in some terrible disaster. It is no wonder that almost immediately folk are moved to take out their chequebooks and credit cards to support a fund for relief to these distressed people.

What concerns me is the unfairness of this very natural and admirable reaction when every day almost 100 people are killed on our roads without any recognition. I suppose that all of us know of someone who has suffered or lost a loved one in a dreadful motor accident - just an individual fatality here and a serious injury there, yet the numbers involved are so great. In the year 2000, 3409 people were killed by road accidents in Great Britain, (one of the safest years on the roads since records began in 1926.) The number of traffic accident casualties was a staggering 320,283. If one adds to that the people who die of accidents each year in the home and in the work place, altogether over 7000 lives are lost each year. Just think of it. Seven thousand precious lives are missing from loving families with all their future promise and potential cut off prematurely. It is equivalent to the inhabitants of a small town like my own cherished place of abode, bordering the New Forest, being wiped out entirely. Any measures that can reduce this horrific number must, of course, be the desire of everyone but my particular concern today is the unfairness that these lives are nationally forgotten. Unfortunately, being isolated tragic incidents they are, largely, only reported in the local press and at the most may raise a paragraph in the nationals. Of course, to the families involved, the grief is just as heartbreaking and debilitating as for those involved in the major disasters, but the sympathy of the public is as fragmented as the tragedies themselves. Loved ones bear their grief alone and unnoticed whilst survivors, watched over by their anxious relatives, either recover with scarring to mind and body, or die and often hardly get a mention in the local paper.

It seems to me that a high profile disaster, however tragic, is no more worthy of generous financial support from the sympathetic public than the individual tragedies that occur daily.

What I would like to see is a general disaster fund that is always open. Every time the hearts of people are moved by a particular tragedy, part of the money given goes to this fund. I don't believe that the amount given would be less because of this arrangement because there would be many who would be prepared to give more, knowing that it would be well spread.

I am aware that there may be difficulties in administration and it may take some years for the fund to become large enough for it to be useful. Nevertheless I can't see why clever people couldn't work out a satisfactory system which in time could bring some relief to the thousands of unheard bearers of pain and grief.

It has been known, in the past, where gigantic funds have been raised in the aftermath of a tragedy for the whole community to be split into factions as various interests assert their claims, which are rejected or modified by the administrators. I think that the proposal I have made would most likely reduce this.

Some might argue that this idea destroys people's freedom to give to what they choose. Surely, knowing that a substantial amount would be available for the particular people who moved them to compassion would satisfy most and some may be prompted to give more, knowing that the balance would be used for the benefit of other tragic victims. In any case, they would know before giving that only so much of the total raised would go to that fund. Grieving folk will often say that nothing can compensate them for their loss, but it would help for them to know that people out of compassion had given to help their needs also. Of course the fund could be open to donations continually and could even have its own special "flower" day.

My hope is that sooner or later an MP will adopt the bare bones of my suggestion as a Private Members Bill with "all party" support, and a General Tragedy Fund to help all families and survivors of accidents and disasters in the UK will become part of our legislation.

(I am sorry if this article has caused distress to anyone but I feel I must say what is on my mind albeit I have been told already that the idea is sound in theory but impractical. I am encouraged that this has been said of many reforming acts.)

Epilogue

I suppose that it is the same with all writers. One is never satisfied, for every time you read the manuscript you see paragraphs which could be worded better or you wonder whether you ought to have included some stories at all, either because they are so personal or maybe are treating a serious subject too flippantly. One good friend didn't like a particular story because he thought that it "humiliated" the writer. Although I understood his concern, I have included this story because when I used it in a broadcast there were favourable comments, including those of the recording engineer, so maybe others will recognise the "nugget" of truth it conveyed.

Some of the stories occurred in a bygone age and critics may claim that because they are old-fashioned they have lost their relevancy for today. My experience with children and young people is that, regardless of advancing technology and a revolution in pop culture, they still warm to stories which reflect the same emotions and feelings as they experience.

However the time for assembling and correcting has passed. I have decided to publish and I pray that the reader will understand that behind every story is an ordinary sort of guy who sometimes messes things up, makes mistakes and is often ashamed. Yet he happens to see in everyday events a reality, a truth which lights him up inside and causes him to be thankful that there is a God who has not despaired of him or the world.

I do hope that you have enjoyed reading these parables and that they have enriched, uplifted and challenged you.

All that Glitters is not Gold

I was trying to design the cover for this book but didn't have a nugget of gold so I screwed up a piece of gold shiny paper and inserted it into the nutshell and photographed it . The result was quite good but when I told our son he said, "You can't use that, dad, especially for a religious book, it's being dishonest". So suitably admonished I decided to try and get hold of a real nugget of gold. The opportunity came when we were in Alaska and I bought a nugget at a very reasonable price.

When I got home I set about photographing the nugget in the shell. Using a star filter and a bright spotlight I looked through the view finder. The result, with shafts of light sparkling from the nugget, was perfect. However the resulting photograph was disappointing. I tried polishing the nugget, photographing it in sun light and using a different camera with no improvement. Why couldn't I reproduce the result apparent in the viewfinder? I don't know. What was I to do for the dead line was approaching?

I must confess I cheated. From some gold paper I cut the smallest diamond shape, less then a millimetre in length, and stuck it on the pointed end of the nugget. The resulting photo was just as I had been seeing it in the viewer and I was delighted.

The question was should I divulge my trickery or should I "come clean"? I haven't yet told our son - he might not approve and I must get this to the printers! Perhaps I should write one last story which has a "nugget in a nutshell" and pacify my conscience at the same time.

Of course the moral is "All that Glitters is not Gold". This well known phrase is taken from Shakespeare's Merchant of Venice the original being "All that Glisters is not Gold". It means that appearances can be deceptive and things that look or sound valuable can be worthless.

I hope, despite the duplicity involved, that the glossy cover of this book will reflect the worth of its contents.

Scriptural Index

General Index

General Index

General Index

General Index